The Adventures of Xavier Winfield *and* His Pal Oggie

by

Roger Smi~~th~~

~ ~ ~ ~ ~ ~ ~

EPISODE ONE

"The Great Camping Adventure"

~ ~ ~ ~ ~ ~ ~

backpack publishers

PO Box 31~ South Webster, OH 45682
www.backpackpublishers.com
A Backpack Inc. Company

Cover Illustration by Taylor Langdon

Library of Congress TXu-783-993
ISBN Number: 978-0-9854439-0-0

ACKNOWLEDGEMENT

I would like to graciously thank my wife for her patience during the long tedious hours when at times it seemed like the boys were never going to make it to the end of their first adventure.

Many thanks also to Alison Witzeman, Alessia Scoccia, Katelynn Selby, and The McCoy family, for their kind words, comments, encouragement, and for their laborious efforts reading and joining me on the road to adventure with Xavier and Oggie. A special thanks also to fellow writer and avid reader, Penny D'Souza, for her wonderful assistance in critiquing characters and storyline.

To each and every reader of this adventure, take life *not* for granted; but as an *opportunity* to find adventure in every step of your own lives.

Roger Smith, Author

Fall 2012

TABLE OF CONTENTS

AUTHOR'S NOTE ABOUT THE USE OF *ITALICS*

Throughout this book there are words in *italics*. The purpose of these *italics* is two-fold in nature:

1. To place emphasis on or highlight to a specific word or subject matter in a particular sentence or paragraph; *and,*

2. To indicate that a word might be in the *Glossary* at the end of the book with pronunciation and definition. This glossary will help younger readers to instantly look the word up in the back of the book and thereby adding to their vocabulary while making the reading more interesting for more mature readers.

It is the authors' intent to provide both an entertainment value and educational experience for each reader regardless of age.

Backpack Publishers

Disclosure – While some of the contents of this book may have been inspired by real events, the characters and story herein are completely fictional and any likeness or representation to real persons or events would be purely coincidental.

The Adventures of Xavier Winfield

and His Pal Oggie

by

Roger Smith

EPISODE ONE

"The Great Camping Adventure"

Sophia,

May your own adventures
be all you want them to be!

Roy Smith

CHAPTER 1

THE DISCOVERY

Xavier (ZAY-vee-err) was an incredibly curious young boy who lived in the large house behind me. When his family moved here, I quickly discovered that this thin, lanky, browned haired, brown eyed boy in glasses, had a curiosity that was second only to his wit; and, for a boy of 11, he seemed to have the academic *maturity* of a well-learned adult. Furthermore, Xavier was quickly *acclaimed* as second to none in our small community when it came to imagination, or should I say, stirring excitement.

Why, I remember that summer that Xavier and his friend Oggie (AWE-gie or Augie), decided to go on a camping *adventure*. Notice that I said *adventure* and not just merely a camping *trip* or *expedition*, for you see, there is a reason. With Xavier, every aspect of life was an opportunity of discovery and *adventure*. In his life, nothing was taken for granted; every moment was something special. And no matter what *adventure* Xavier was tackling, he was sure to include his chunky shorter than average 10 year old, freckle faced, red curly headed, neighbor friend Oggie. Yes, that camping adventure was an experience to remember I tell you; and, as a former teacher, their esteemed neighbor, and good friend to both boys *and* their parents, I remember every incident that those boys encountered, for they loved including me in all their travels, *escapades*, and tales. Why, let me see if I can recall the events of the camping *adventure* and you'll soon see what I mean.

"Oggie, help me up in the rafters," shouted the slender narrow faced little boy, as he was stretching his hands higher to reach the rafters of the shed he and his friend Oggie were exploring.

"Your gonna fall," short and pudgy firm Oggie replied.

Xavier and Oggie were exploring a storage shed that was behind Xavier's grandpa and grandma's house. This storage shed was one of those buildings with weathered lumber, having a gabled roof and a few small paned windows. It had a shabby looking door that was well weathered, and a metal latch with a stick inserted to keep the door closed. To see out of the few small windows one would have to wipe away years of film and dust from the small glass squares to even venture a look outside. Anyway, this particular building housed the storage contents of Xavier's grandpa and grandma Winfield's forgotten surplus.

"Hurry Oggie," shouted Xavier, motioning to Oggie with his left hand. Xavier was standing on some old wooden boxes that he had piled on top of each other to make a tall pillar of stairs. The largest box was on the bottom and the boxes decreased in size as they stacked higher. This stacked arrangement, created a staircase for Xavier to climb up in the rafters. At the top of the pile, Xavier's left foot tiptoed on the stack, while his right leg dangled in the air, trying to lift and also thrust himself upward. With his right arm extended flat on some planks that straddled the rafters in the gable of this almost forgotten hideaway, Xavier summoned for help.

"Push me up!" He shouted impatiently, scrambling to boost himself up on the planks.

"O.K.! O.K.!" Oggie spouted back jumping to action to serve the needs of his best friend. Oggie grabbed hold of Xavier's left leg and pushed. With one fast projection, the light-weighted slender Xavier popped up on the planks, sending down a cloud of formerly undisturbed dust, which now landed on the face, head, and shoulders of one Oglethorpe (OH-gull-thorp) Bartholomew, a shorter than average, slightly overweight, sandy red hear10 year old peppered with freckles.

"Man!" Oggie exclaimed as he wiped his face and dusted off. "What are you gonna do up there?"

"I wanta' see what's up here."

"Ahh-choo!" Oggie's body responded violently to the powdery dust.

"Sorry Og," snapped Xavier, as he, on all fours maneuvered around the junk in the top of the gabled building.

"It's O.K.," his friend replied, "ahh-choo! Anything up there?" Asked Oggie wiping his nose on his shirtsleeve.

"Yeah. Looks like a tent and some camping gear." Xavier slid some things around and hollered.

"Look out below!" He said.

Oggie jumped back as a large dusty bag came crashing to the floor. With one end of the bag opened, a dull green canvas tent slightly protruded out of one end.

"Ah-choo! I gotta get outta here."

"Hold up Oggie," shouted Xavier, "there's all kinds of campin' gear up here. Catch!" In his one hand he waved a drab green canteen and in the other an army green backpack. Oggie quickly reached his hands in the air for the catch as his attic friend let loose of the canteen. With a good catch, Oggie quickly dropped the canteen to the floor and readied himself for the backpack. Just as Xavier released the pack, Oggie threw his head back, squinted his eyes, and threw his head forward.

"Ahhh-chhoo!" He screamed. The backpack struck the bent over Oggie on the back of the head, sending him to the floor nearly unconscious.

"Oggie! You OK?" Shouted Xavier; however, there was no response.

Frightened out of his wits, Xavier quickly lowered himself through the rafters and jumped to the floor with a crash and scrambled to his friends' side. He knelt over his ten-year-old buddy, who was almost lifeless and repeated his inquiry.

"You all right Oggie? Say something! Please be all right! Oggie!"

"Cool it man, I'm O.K.. Yer breakin' my ear drums!" Oggie squinted his eyes and leaned up on one elbow and shouted, "I gotta get outta here I tell ya!"

"Sure," comforted Xavier as he helped his short plump playmate up and out the door.

"Here, blow your nose," said Xavier, handing Oggie his own red patterned handkerchief after removing his gold-rimmed eyeglasses and wiping them clean adding, "You O.K.?"

"I think. I Just got a bunch of dust," said Oggie as he snorted and grunted into Xavier's handkerchief.

Confident that his friend was O.K., Xavier's eyes quickly shifted from his friend back into the shed where the backpack had spilled open as it had hit Oggie and the floor.

"Wow, look at all the stuff," shouted Xavier. He quickly hurled back into the shed, sorting through all the *paraphernalia*. Oggie meanwhile, continued to clear his nasal passages of the dust.

"Look, here's a compass." Xavier knelt beside the backpack and held up a compass toward Oggie.

"Ahh-choo! Let me see," shouted Oggie, perking to life and shifting his attention back inside where Xavier was holding up a round green object. Oggie quickly sprang into motion nearly bouncing back into the shed with inquisitive excitement, where he knelt down beside Xavier, who was now engrossed in the usage of this newfound device.

"Hey look, what's this funny looking thing." Oggie had picked up a green colored metal object that resembled a flying saucer.

"That's a mess kit Oggie," snorted Xavier, taking the object from his friend. And, pulling the kit up close to his face with a few inquisitive looks and a couple twists of some metal

4

hooks, the seemingly useless metal object transformed into a skillet and a plate, in which also were a fork, knife and spoon.

"See?" He handed the disassembled mess kit to Oggie.

"Gee, this is neat. Wonder if your grandpa will let us use this stuff?"

Xavier looked up from what he was examining and gazed toward a corner of the building as if he were slipping into a trance. Oggie twisted his body around to examine what it was that warranted Xavier's stare, expecting to see Xavier's grandfather although there was no one. Looking back to Xavier, Oggie's forehead wrinkled with suspicion as he gazed on his friend, the latter of who now looked as though he were far, far away. Oggie turned his attention back to digging out the next item and between examinations of the newfound devices; he would occasionally look up at Xavier wondering what had captured his friends' attention. Oggie even once again looked in the direction of Xavier's stare and was just getting ready to ask what was wrong.

"Come on." Shouted Xavier jumping up past his stocky little friend and patting him on the back, "I have an idea."

Xavier sprinted toward the door of the shed carrying the compass.

"What's up man?" Questioned Oggie while he *maneuvered* himself to his feet still holding the mess kit.

"I got an idea. Bring the canteen."

Xavier sprang out the door and touched ground about six feet from the building, then headed toward the back door of his grandparents house. Oggie dropped the mess kit and grabbed the canteen and headed for the door. He jumped out the shed door also, not advancing quite as far as his light-footed companion, and worked hard at trying to keep up.

"Where we goin?" Asked Oggie with curiosity trailing Xavier about ten to twelve feet. Xavier stopped dead in his tracks just before reaching the back door and spun around.

"I'm gonna ask grandpa if we can use this camping gear and go on a camping expedition. What'da ya think?" And without giving Oggie a chance to answer the excited Xaiver continued, "wanna?"

"Sure!" Responded Oggie, his eyes lighting up like he'd just set his eyes on cotton candy for the first time.

CHAPTER 2

THE INQUIRY

The two boys ran inside the back door of the house, the wooden screen door crashing closed behind them.

"That you Xavier?" Uttered the familiar elderly female voice from the living room.

"Yes ma'am. Where's grandpa?"

"How many times have I told you not to slam that door Xavier?"

"Sorry, Ma'am," Xavier ran through the kitchen and into the large country living room where he was sure that his grandma's voice had come from. Entering the room, as he had expected, his grandmother sat in a dark stained rocker in the corner by the fireplace. Her hair was grayed and rolled into a bun tight against the top of her head. She wore small eyeglasses, which hung near the end of her nose, and Xavier had seen her look over them with an evil stare when she would stare through him when searching for the truth.

"Grandpa's upstairs laying down," she reported taking her eyes from the darning work which was inter-tangled between darning needles and her hands. The yarn ran along her right arm and to the floor alongside the rocker where there was a woven cane basket. She leaned forward in the rocker and continued.

"But with your clanging the door, he'll not be sleepin' long." She asserted.

No sooner were those words spoken when they heard the familiar footsteps of someone descending the long staircase from the upstairs bedrooms.

"See Xavier, here he comes now," said she, now resting her hands in her lap and leaning forward to look around the large stone fireplace which protruded out from the wall about two or three feet, and covering about a quarter of the one living room wall.

"Grandpa! Grandpa," shouted Xavier as he hurried directly across the room to the closed door that fronted the stairs to the second floor.

"Hold on cowboy. Hold your horses. I'm comin' down," came that familiar crisp voice behind the slowly opening door, a voice known to Xavier as Grandpa Winfield.

Without heeding the voice of Grandpa Winfield, Xavier inquired, "Is that your campin' gear in the shed?"

Emerging from the doorway, the tall slender white haired elderly man ducked to clear the doorway.

"What you into now son?" Asked Grandpa Winfield.

"There's a bunch of camping gear in the shed and it's neat." Xavier grabbed his grandfathers' left hand and started tugging, "come on we'll show you."

The lean giant of a man leaned toward the inquisitive Xavier, smiled through his neatly trimmed Clark Gable mustache.

"Sure lead the way cowboy."

"Harold, what about your medicine?" Grandma Winfield questioned.

"There'll be time for that grandma," said he looking back to his right toward where she was sitting, as an ever-anxious Xavier was dragging him.

"I shan't be long." With that, he and the boys disappeared into the kitchen and out the back door.

Just as the three emerged the rear screen door, Grandpa Winfield quickly turned and reached back to grab the screen door just before it was about to crash against the door enclosure.

"Gramma.....," started Grandpa Winfield.

"Yep. Forgot." said Xavier, tugging on the ole man's left hand with more intensity.

"Relax critter, I'll go with you."

As the party arrived at the shed, Xavier jumped the single step into the building, while Grandpa Winfield stepped one foot on the first step and leaned forward putting his hands on the upper part of his leg to assist the entry by pushing his torso forward, one step at a time until he had maneuvered the step and was inside.

Xavier dropped to his knees in a forward slide stopping in front of the backpack and other *paraphernalia* that cluttered the floor.

"Look at this neat ole compass, grandpa. Is it yours?" Without giving Grandpa Winfield a chance to answer, Xavier continued, "Did you used to use it? Did you ever camp out with this stuff?"

The old man pulled over an old paint faded, weathered, wooden chair and sat down reaching for the compass that Xavier was handing up toward him. As he took hold of the compass from Xavier he chuckled.

" Where'd ya' find this 'stuff', as you call it?" Asked Grandpa Winfield.

"It was up there," said Xaiver pointing to the small loft that ceilinged the back half of the shed.

"I forgot about this gear. Your Dad and I used to camp with this Xavier. We'd go on fishing trips for a day or two. Your Dad treasured the time we spent together and we always had some tale to come back with."

"Did ya' catch anything? And did ya' cook your catch in this?" Ask Oggie, lifting the mess kit.

"Sure did, and we had to take turns cooking and eating cause we only had this one kit."

"Why didn't ya' get another one, grandpa?" Xavier's forehead crinkled with inquisition.

"Times were bad Xavier. We didn't have money for a second one. But, it didn't seem to worry us none though. Your Dad an' I never paid no mind to it. We just enjoyed the outdoors and the hiking and fishin'. It was a joyful time."

"Did Dad catch any big ones?"

"Oh boy, did he! One time he snagged this big ole channel cat that was about a foot an' a half long. I'd had a big line on yer Dad's rod and when that cat struck, he jerked the rod right outta yer Dad's hands." The old man rested back in his chair shaking his head to and fro and chuckling.

"Xavier your pop was so excited that he jumped in the water and grabbed the rod. You shoulda' seen the look on his face. It was like he was sayin', 'boy I just did a stupid, huh?' Well, I hollered at him to pull it in, and your Dad fought that baby for what seemed like half an hour, but it was really only a couple minutes."

Grandpa Winfield leaned forward and started laughing. Xavier and Oggie joined in and started laughing too.

"What happened next?" asked Xavier.

"Well, when yer Dad caught a glimpse of the size of that cat, he jumped outta the water and screamed for me to take the rod. I told him go ahead and pull it in. But yer Dad was too scared, so I took the rod and reeled it in. Boy, you should have seen your pop's eyes when that cat came in. They were as big as saucers. He told everybody in town how he reeled in the biggest catfish in the county."

"Man, wait'll I tell Dad!"

"Yeah, you tell him. An' ask him if there's ever been a cat that big caught in these parts since. He'll tell ya' all right! Boy was he shocked."

"Grandpa, could you take us campin' and fishing'?" Xavier pleaded.

"Oh boy would that be great or what?" Oggie jumped up excitedly, "Can I go too?"

Before Grandpa Winfield could grasp the question, Xavier turned to Oggie and spouted.

"You bet man." Xavier then turned to his grandpa and added, "Oggie can go to right?"

The old man stretched his hands out in front of him and motioned, STOP.

"Now hold on a minute boys. Nobody said anything about goin' campin'. You'd have to have more than this stuff. You need food, a first aid kit, toilet paper, and a whole lot more."

"We can get that stuff at the store," said Oggie.

"An' where ya gonna get the money?" Grandpa inquired.

The boys turned their visual focus from Grandpa Winfield to each other to think on what he had just asked, when suddenly Xavier drew a brainstorm.

"We'll collect pop bottles and turn 'em in to get enough money to buy everything we need," Xavier said shaking his head up and down as if to get Grandpa Winfield to agree to the idea.

Interrupting the conversation the three heard the intruding voice of Grandma Winfield from the direction of the house.

"Harold; your medicine. You have to take them on schedule." Her voice sounded almost pleading.

Grandpa Winfield handed Xavier the compass and using his hands on his upper legs to lift himself up, turned toward the door and hollered toward the house.

"Be right there, Puggs."

Xavier smiled hearing the old man call his wife that name, remembering that Grandpa had nicknamed her that when they were going together before they were married and only used it on occasion as a sort of term of *endearment*.

"Well, you boys work on that camping idea, all right?" With that he slumped humbly out the door, ducking his head down and to the left as he stepped downward and slowly disappeared out of their sight.

"Wow, Xavier! I can't wait. Let's go start collecting bottles now!"

Getting up, Xavier instructed his little comrade, "we'll use your red wagon, and we're gonna need a lot of bottles. Maybe fifty or a hundred."

"Let's do it!" And with that, the boys were out the door.

CHAPTER 3

THE PLAN

So, for the remainder of the day Xavier and Oggie took Oggie's red wagon and collected pop bottles along the two state highways and the few busy streets that checkerboard patterned their small village of Chestnut Ridge. Chestnut Ridge was one of those wide spots in the road that was merely a stopping place along the way between two larger towns gone by. Now lazily resting for nearly two decades, the village had depleted its' population to around 2,000 from its heyday of nearly double that when the coal industry was strong.

By evenings end, the two boys had managed to navigate and search both the state highways that intersected their village and all major streets in town, returning to the Winfield home by early afternoon. In all, they had collected enough bottles to raise $11.83. Then, back at the shed that evening, the two boys sat down and surveyed their financial gain for the day.

"What should we get with our money?" Oggie inquired of his thinker buddy.

"Well, let's see...," responded Xavier lifting his left hand to his chin pondering their needs and gazing off deep in thought. Oggie sat with his legs crossed, each elbow on a knee, cradling his chin and staring at the thinker. Xavier's eyes opened a little wider and jumped to attention. Oggie jerked back.

"What is it?" He asked.

Xavier responded, "I'll be right back," and headed for door to exit the shed.

"What's up, Xav? (ZAY-va)" Oggie twisted to see his buddy shoot out the door.

"Be right back," trailed Xavier's voice and he was gone.

It was just a few seconds and Oggie heard the screen door crash closed and that familiar distant voice echo.

"Xavier!"

Panting, Xavier shouted back, "Sorry Ma'am," and Oggie knew that Xavier had again forgotten to catch the screen door. While Xavier was absent, Oggie pondered why Xavier could not remember a little detail like catching a closing screen door, and yet could quote the Gettysburg Address, Preamble to the Constitution verbatim, and also understand and use algebraic formulas and chemistry. Surely remembering the door was not so complex he thought.

Xavier zoomed in through the shed door and retook the place, where he had been before leaving, his arrival pre-announced by the slamming sound of the kitchen screen door, followed by Grandma Winfield's scolding voice. In his hands was a tablet and pen.

"We'll make a list of everything we need."

"Hey, great idea," said Oggie, thinking of how Xavier thought of everything.

"Food," Xavier penned a title and drew a line under it.

"Potato chips," added Oggie.

"No Oggie, we gotta have good foods. We don't want to get sick. We need nutritious foods," scolded Xavier.

"Shoot this ain't gonna be any fun at all."

"Oggie we wanna show our parents that we know how to handle ourselves so they'll trust us. What do ya' think?"

"Yeah, I guess your right," said Oggie, slumping his chin into hand.

"Don't ya think we oughta ask our moms and dads?"

"Not yet," said Xavier, "we'll wait till we got all the stuff together and they'll feel we're showing mature *judgment*, and they'll feel *obligated* to let us take a shot at it. What'd you think?"

Perking up to Xavier's brainstorm, Oggie lifted his head opening his eyes real wide.

"Yeah, Xav. Great idea. You think of everything. I wish I were half as smart as you."

The two boys held thumbs up at each other to show their agreement with each other and continued with their task at hand.

CHAPTER 4

THE LIST

"Vegetables. Canned of course." Xavier began penning the list, "green beans, pork & beans, mixed vegetables, and what else?"

"Corn," Oggie inserted, licking his lips with anticipation of his favorite vegetable.

"Sure, and carrots too."

"Yuck!" Oggie snarled his lips up against his nose.

"Mom's will like it, Og."

"Oh yeah, yer right."

Before sundown, the boys had penned out the remainder of the list:

Food	Drinks	Other	Tools
green beans	kool Aide	adhesive tape	hunting knives
pork n beans	pop	band aids	hatchet
mixed veg		gauze	string
corn		newspaper	army shovel
carrots		kites	small canvas

Camping Gear	Clothes	Other Tools
tent	underwear	BB guns
compass	socks	sling shot
canteens	tee shirts	
sleeping bags	jean shorts	
mess kit		

"There, I think we've got everything. But if we've forgotten something, we can always add it. You have to make a list or else you'll never remember everything," said Xavier folding up the list and putting it in his pocket, "how long do ya' think we should ask to go?"

"How about a month," perked Oggie, jumping to his feet.

Xavier stood up and frowned, "c'mon Og, do you really think our moms and dads are gonna allow us to camp out away from home a whole month?"

"Well......I guess not. But, how 'bout a couple weeks?"

"Let's ask for three or four days and we'll leave Thursday. What'da ya say?"

"But that's the day after tomorrow. Let's go tomorrow," said Oggie anxiously.

"Well, don't ya' think we ought to get our supplies together tomorrow first?" Xavier pointed out to his buddy.

"Well, guess you're right Xav," responded Oggie as he picked up the canteen and unscrewed the lid and squinted a look inside.

"But I sure wished we could go tomorrow." Added Oggie.

"Me too, Og. But, we ought to be prepared and have all our supplies for our expedition. And, ya know," Xavier's conversation was interrupted by Oggie tossing the canteen across the shed after acting like he was going to take a drink from it.

"PHEW!!" That thing stinks," said Oggie snarling his nose and shaking his head to the left and right, "I'm not gonna drink anything outta that."

Xavier laughed and reached down to pick up the canteen where it had landed after bouncing off the shed wall. "We'll clean it up first, brainless."

"You'll never get rid'o that smell. Something must have died in there."

Xavier held the metal canister up toward his nose and sniffed carefully the disgusting smell then jerked it away quickly with a frown.

"I think it's spoiled milk."

"You sure?" Inquired Oggie intently.

"Yep, sure is. Smells just like that milk I gave my sister Natty when she was little and she got sick."

Oggie took the canteen from Xavier and carefully raised it to his head, again holding his head back while doing so, and sniffing short sniffs.

"Smell; it smells like that formula stuff," continued Xavier.

"Yeah. That stuff stunk," agreed Oggie snarling his nose once more and shaking his head in agreement. "How come you gave that stuff to her Xav?"

"I thought it was that formula stuff."

"Oh yeah. That stuff stunk too," Oggie shook his head in affirmation.

"Let's get all our stuff together and go ask to go," said Xavier as he started packing everything into a green canvas backpack.

"Who we gonna ask first, Xav?" Asked Oggie handing Xavier some of the supplies which were laying all about around him, as Xavier knelt back down to pack up some of the gear.

"Who would you go to first?" Asked Xavier, getting up on his feet.

"How 'bout your grandpa and grandma first?" Oggie pointed out, maneuvering his extra weight to get upward.

"Why?" Asked Xavier as if to acquire the reasoning of his friend.

Oggie thought carefully so as not to look like a fool in front of his friend. For, he knew full well that Xavier had already made his choice and his reasons for his choice. So, after some thought, Oggie responded with a puzzled look.

"I don't know?"

"Could it be that you think your mom and dad will be more likely to let you go if my mom and dad say O.K.?" Inquired Xavier.

"Yeah, that's it! Uh huh, that's it. That's what I was thinking." Fibbed he. As Oggie powered that fib back, he cleared the puzzled look from his face. Both boys knew that Oggie really hadn't reasoned this, but the response being simply triggered by Xavier's already witted summation.

"Let's go talk to grandpa first," Xavier looked serious; then, with the back of his hand tapped Oggie on the chest, got up, and headed straight for the door. Oggie quickly maneuvered himself up and followed Xaiver straight away behind him looking up a head's height to Xavier.

"By the way, how's come?" Asked Oggie.

Xavier stopped, spun around back toward Oggie, as the latter nearly crashed into the back of his friend, and stepping back Xavier answered.

"You'll see." Having said that, he went out the shed door heading for the back door to the kitchen with Oggie hot on his trail.

CHAPTER 5

THE REQUEST

The boys scooted in the back door with Xavier in the lead and Oggie close behind. As they entered, the telephone rang. Oggie had just cleared the threshold of the kitchen door, when Xavier jammed dead in his tracks and swung back at Oggie.

"Get the screen!" Xavier shouted.

Oggie jumped back and caught the screen just before it crashed against the door jam. Both boys looked at each other square in the eyes and measured a sigh of relief over their faces knowing that they had just avoided a scolding.

"WHEW! That was close," said Oggie.

"Way ta' go, Og."

Entering the living room, they quietly went over to grandpa Winfield who was sitting in his reclining rocker reading the afternoon newspaper. Grandma Winfield was on the telephone talking about a church bazaar, which signaled to Xavier that they just might have seized the perfect moment.

"Grandpa, would you take us camping?" Xavier asked softly to avoid Grandma Winfield from hearing the conversation, then looking at Oggie beside him. Oggie's face screwed up with question. Grandpa Winfield lowered the paper to his lap and looked over his glasses.

"Now there's an interesting thought," he responded.

"What'da ya mean," the young boy inquired.

"Well, I sure would like to do that...." Before Harold Winfield could continue, Xavier jumped back and clapped his hands with glee like a boy of five or six, Oggie nearly mirroring Xavier's actions.

"Hold on a minute Xavier. I hadn't finished," continued grandpa Winfield.

"Huh?" Questioned Xavier.

"What I was about to say, is that I would love to camp out with you boys, but your grandma would never allow it," he chuckled then added, "Besides, at 70 I suppose that I'd not be able to walk for a week if I was to sleep on the ground."

"Ah, c'mon grandpa?" Pleaded Xavier.

"Yeah, Mr. Winfield, please?" Added Oggie.

"I'm sorry boys, but I'm just too old."

"You're never too old grandpa."

"Sorry boys. But I'll just have to say no."

"Well, would ya care if we went campin'?" Asked Xavier.

Grandpa tilted his head a little to the right and forward and inquired of Xavier.

"How could you go camping if I don't go?"

"Well," Xavier moved closer to the old man and chose his words carefully.

"You know that Oggie and I have camped out in the back yard before?"

"You sure have," he responded.

"And, you know that Oggie and I know the woods behind the old farm house," referring to the woods behind the old abandoned Winfield farm at the north end of town. The farm had been the family homestead where Grandpa Winfield had been raised as a boy, but had been abandoned some 15 years ago when great grandma Winfield passed away and the land had been strip mined for coal. The old homestead house had been sold and was relocated nearly four miles further north about two years earlier on the main state road that runs north and south through Chestnut Ridge. Xavier had loved watching the crews lift and move the house with all that heavy-duty equipment. He was amazed that a *"whole house,"* as he put it, could be moved down the road. However, Grandpa Winfield and Xavier's dad often took the boys on walks or hikes there and Xavier and Oggie regularly hiked the woods behind the old Winfield home.

"Yep, I guess that if anyone knows those woods, it'd be you critters," remarked Xavier's grandpa as his eyes shifted above the boys and to the left as he dazed into a time of the past. Oggie, standing to the right of Xavier, looked behind and above as if to look for the object of grandpa Winfield's stare.

"Well," Xavier pressed carefully, "I was just thinking that we could clean up all that camping gear we found in the shed, if it'd be all right? And then, since we already sold pop bottles and bought food and supplies for the trip..."

Xavier paused his plea and reached into his pocket and pulled out the crumbled camping supply list and handed it to grandpa Winfield.

"See what we got?" He asked.

"Yeah, look at all the stuff we bought from selling pop bottles," added Oggie.

"So, that's what you boys been up to. I seen ya pushing that wagon with boxes in it," remarked Mr. Winfield as he looked over the list handed him.

"Sure looks thorough Xavier. What ever gave you boys this idea?"

"Well," added Xavier, moving in for the kill, "we haven't had anything to do constructive since my mom and dad went left for the trip to Ireland with my sister Natalie to take care of uncle Thomas while he's sick, and so we thought that we ought to put our minds and hands to something worthwhile."

Xavier knew that his grandpa always sought work over idleness. He'd heard his grandpa tell stories about his years working hard on the farm.

"Well, such a camping trip would keep you boys busy, that's for sure."

Aiming for the juggler vein, as Xavier had heard his parents say often when aiming for the kill shot in any argument or decisive conversation, Xavier thus zeroed his aim on the final target.

"I knew that's what you'd want for us grandpa." He added.

Oggie turned to Xavier with a puzzled look. Xavier winked at Oggie out of Grandpa Winfield's line of eyesight and tapped Oggie on the left hip and nodded for Oggie to turn his face toward grandpa Winfield.

"Let's see what grandma Winfield thinks?" Nodded Grandpa Winfield.

Xavier knew that talking to grandma Winfield had to be avoided. Grandma Winfield would never go for the idea.

"Grandpa?" Asked Xavier proceeding with cautious precision and carefully chosen words.

"Grandma would never understand things that us guys know are necessary to learn about life and growing up, right?"

"Well, I understand that idea, Xavier," grandpa Winfield responded. "I do believe you boys would sure enjoy yourselves."

Having learned that when a grown up was mostly in agreement one had better take affirmative action before the adult says, 'of course on the other hand...,' and thus Xavier quickly leaned forward to hug his grandpa.

"Gee, thanks grandpa, I knew you'd want us to learn all the valuable experiences in life." Touted Xavier cheerfully.

"Let's go see if you can go, Oggie." And with that the two boys were out the back door with the bang of the slamming screen behind them. They both stopped dead in their tracks, looked back, and stretched the corner of their mouths with a frown as they together cringed their shoulders as the crashing sound echoed in their skulls, following which they shrugged their shoulders and headed off for Oggie's house quickly.

CHAPTER 6

THE PLEA

At Oggie's, things weren't going quite as well as at the Winfield's.

"But why not mom?" Pleaded Oggie with his hands together as if he were praying, "please?"

"Because Oggie, you and Xavier are too young to go on a trip by yourselves." Mrs. Bartholomew was washing the dishes and the clanging of pots and pans in water pierced her conversation.

After only a few moments of conversational exchange between Oggie and his mother, Xavier entered the conversation at the appropriate moment.

"Mrs. Bartholomew, if I could engage your attention for just a moment, I believe that I can clear up your concerns," asked Xavier politely.

To that address, the young attractive aged thirties Mrs. Bartholomew stopped what she was doing then shook the water from her hands into the sink, and began drying her hands with the apron attached around her waist as she turned toward the addressing Xavier; she leaned back against the counter and put both hands on her waist.

"I swear Xavier, there are times that I have to remind myself that you are only a child. Come on, let's sit down and you boys tell me the whole scoop. Would you boys like some fresh chocolate chip cookies?" Said she as the boys' focus turned from camping to that sweet warm aroma that had been teasing the boys' nostrils the moment they entered the room;

but dared not talk about cookies when approval on a camping trip was what they sought.

"Sure!" Both boys resounded instantly.

"Just one, because you boys will be eating in a little while."

"Yes ma'am," they echoed together.

The boys quickly moved to the large round oak kitchen table that sat in the center of the kitchen. Before examining the possibilities of where to sit, Xavier reached into the large cookie jar handed him by Mrs. Bartholomew, and pulled out a nice sized chocolate chip cookie with lots of chocolate chips exposed and instantly took a bite. Between bites and munching Xavier squeezed out a quick word.

"Thank you ma'am. These are great!" Oggie followed with Xavier's offer of thanks as well.

"You're welcome boys," said Mrs. Bartholomew returning the large ceramic cookie jar to the kitchen counter where she had gotten it.

"Wow, these are warm and really good!" Exclaimed Xavier licking his lips and flashing his upper eyebrows up and down.

"You're too much Xavier. Thank you."

The boys quickly moved to the table and Xavier pulled out one of the high back chairs from the table and offered it to Mrs. Bartholomew for a seat. Then, each boy sat on either side of Mrs. Bartholomew, positioning themselves carefully so that she could only see one or the other at a time, and never both.

"Why thank you Xavier. You boys must really want this trip." Mrs. Bartholomew pulled her long brown hair back with both her hands by covering her face with both hands and pushing them back over her head.

Oggie started to talk and his mother turned her head toward him. Xavier motioned outside the vision of Mrs. Bartholomew a suggestive waving hand and gritting teeth that Oggie should shut his mouth, which Oggie did.

"Well, it's like this Mrs. Bartholomew," said Xavier putting his spread fingertips together in front of him while touching his lips with his index finger and resting his elbows on the tabletop. Mrs. Bartholomew turned her head to the right to gaze upon Xavier, who looked quite like the *proverbial* judge while pondering a witness' testimony.

"Oggie and I found this camping gear in grandpa's shed out back and we cleaned it all up and got this idea for a short camping trip at our family farm. We wrote out a plan and here it is." Xavier reached in his pocket and pulled out the crumpled list and unfolded it while also handing it to Mrs. Bartholomew.

Mrs. Bartholomew reached out to receive the unfolded paper.

"My you boys have been busy. I wondered where you've been Oggie." She then unfolded the paper and gazed upon the writing therein.

"Well, you see Mrs. Bartholomew," she raised her eyes from the paper Xavier had handed her and cracked a smile looking at Xavier with amazement.

"We calculated how much money we'd need, then collected pop bottles using Oggie's wagon and we already got our supplies." He continued.

"My. My. I'm impressed."

"Then, when grandpa Winfield said he thought it was a good idea, we were sure that you'd be happy that we are doing something constructive with our idle time and energy."

"Oh, grandpa Winfield thinks it's a good idea?" She asked, her eyes perking back demonstrating an expression of relief.

"Yes ma'am. He said he thinks we'll enjoy ourselves and he knows we know the woods behind the old Winfield house; well err, where the house used to be because Oggie and I go hiking there all the time." Oggie now jumped in for support.

"Yeah Mom. You know Xav and I go there lots." As Mrs. Bartholomew turned her head toward her son, Xavier frowned at Oggie and put his finger to his lips to instruct Oggie to keep his mouth shut.

"It's true, you two are in those woods often," confirmed Mrs. Bartholomew, then continuing with, "Well I suppose…"

Mrs. Bartholomew leaned back and pondered for a moment before continuing.

"Yeah, I suppose you could get ready for the trip and then we'll run it by your father, Oggie."

Oggie thought to himself, 'that means, NO!'

"That'll be great Mrs. Bartholomew, we can even help you sell the idea to him. So, let us know when you're ready to talk to him."

"Well, I'll be! Xavier, if I didn't know better, I'd say I had just been had."

Not wanting any further discussion along these lines, with a childish, or more correctly put, impish smile, Xavier wanted to exit while they were ahead.

"We really appreciate you Mrs. Bartholomew. And, gee thanks for the cookies." Xavier motioned with his hand low out of Mrs. Bartholomew's view for Oggie to get up and upon Oggie doing so; the boys scurried for the door.

"Thanks Xavier; now outta here both of you. You boys are probably getting me in trouble. If dinner isn't ready when your father gets home Oggie, it will go a long way to kill our, hmmmm I mean *your* plan, huh?" Said she giving a wink and nod to Xavier, who responded thusly with an agreeing nod back.

Oggie's eyes popped as wide as saucers and his cheeks puffed a smile like a squirrel with its' jaws full of nuts.

"Thanks again Mrs. Bartholomew. Let's go Oglethorpe." And with that, Xavier grabbed the camping list and the boys shot out the door leaving Mrs. Bartholomew sitting at the table shaking her head in amazement. Outside the boys cheered their efforts with hand gestures, as they hurried to the shed to finish up the list so they were ready when, and of course if, they received the approval.

"Wow, that was smooth Xav," Oggie panted, taking extra steps to keep stride with his longer legged friend.

"Yea, I think your mom will help sell your dad on the idea. And so, we're on our way!"

CHAPTER 7

LET'S GO

Mrs. Bartholomew explained the boys' camping idea to Mr. Bartholomew fairly clearly at the dinner table, and when he had not answered her inquiry to him directly about the boys going on the trip, she supposed that that he was in approval. Why, in fact, when she had reminded him of *his* first camping trip he had not only not disagreed with the idea but he had even gotten excited and exclaimed, 'Boy I'll bet you boys would have a ball!' Thus, when left the dinner table a short time later without saying, 'no,' she concluded that his silence about the matter was an approval. Regrettably however, Mr. Bartholomew had merely slipped away from the table to daydream of his first camping trip even though Mrs. Bartholomew supposed that the trip was a 'go.'

So, without objections the next day the boys loaded up.

"Well, we're ready!" Oggie perked standing in front of his red wagon that was heaped nearly as high as he was tall. The wagon looked like one of those prepackaged aluminum popcorn canisters that expanded bulky after popping, only decorated in green with an olive drab green tarp.

Xavier sat on the big rock next to the shed and was reviewing the list a second and third time; however, the Tools portion of the list was on the back side of the small piece of paper he was using and had he reviewed that portion of the list more closely he would have noticed that even though they had packed the hatchet, they had forgotten to pack the BB guns, knife, and sling shot and had they noticed those items and packed them, perhaps things forward would have turned out different.

"Seems like we're forgetting something."

"What on earth could it be? We've packed everything we got."

"I don't know, but I'm sure we'll figure it out tonight when we need it," Xavier frowned while folding up the list they had prepared so meticulously. He stuffed it in his pocket and leaned forward to get up from his comfortable position.

"Well, let's go!" Oggie snapped pulling on the tongue of the wagon.

"Og, don't ya think we outta say good-bye?"

Dropping the wagon tongue to the ground, Oggie's lower jaw dropped as he sounded out withdrawn, "oh, yeah."

"I'll say good-bye to grandma and grandpa while you say good-bye to your mom," Xavier instructed.

Continuing he added, "Don't get into a lot of conversation with your mom and whatever you do don't say anything about getting hurt."

"You got it, Xav," and with that Oggie headed toward his house next door.

Xavier's heart started pounding a little faster as he headed for the back door for fear that something would go wrong saying good-bye. He slipped in the back door quietly, adding special care not to let the screen door slam, and tip toed across the kitchen floor listening to the conversation in the living room. Grandma Winfield was hosting a morning quilting 'get together' as was the custom in those days. Xavier listened attentively while the women talked about their men folk. At the appropriate calculated time, he walked into the room where grandma Winfield had just begun to expound on grandpa Winfield's thunderous snoring.

"Oh, there's that handsome young Xavier," Mrs. Thomas expounded stopping her quilting and resting her hand in her lap. The Thomas' owned the hardware store in town, appropriately named THOMAS HARDWARE.

"Well, hi there Xavier," said Joan Jones the widow of the towns first druggist; the store now being run by her son Randy.

"Oh hi Mrs. Jones," responded Xavier turning his head to the right in her direction but continuing directly toward his grandmother in the far corner rocker by the fireplace.

"You're such a polite young man Xavier," she continued.

"Thank you ma'am."

"What do you need Xavier," asked grandma Winfield, stopping her hand quilting work and looking up toward him over her granny glasses.

"I thought I'd watch you for a moment."

"Oh a young boy wouldn't be interested in what we're doin'."

"I just don't see how all those little pieces of cloth turn into a blanket." Said Xavier stopping beside grandma Winfield's chair and looking intently at her work.

"It's just a quilt Xavier," inserted Mrs. Thomas.

Grandma Winfield turned her head toward Xavier shifting her work piece.

"Well, sometime I'll show you how it's done, Xavier, but for now why don't you run along and play. You don't want to hang around here and listen to a bunch of old women gossip do you?" Asked the elder Mrs. Winfield with an aged shaky voice.

"Well, I guess not, but I thought I'd watch for a while before I go. But maybe you're right."

Xavier leaned over and kissed Mrs. Winfield on the cheek.

"See ya later grandma." Xavier paused momentarily before turning toward the door for an exit.

"Your such a fine young man," added Mrs. Thomas.

Grandma Winfield's face turned a little pink flush as she gave him a peck on the cheek.

"Mrs. Thomas was giving you a complement Xavier," said she placing her fragile hand on his shoulder.

"Yes Ma'am. Thank you Mrs. Thomas," Xavier said turning toward Mrs. Thomas and offering a hip height partial wave to her.

"Be seein' ya grandma." Xavier kind of blushed and headed nervously across the room to the doorway leading to the kitchen. Behind him he heard Mrs. Thomas' voice.

"Almost sounds like he's leaving or something." The women chuckled and continued their conversation.

"Oh those boys are always up to something; he and Ogglethorpe, you know the Bartholomew boy next door. Who knows what they're cookin' up today," said grandma Winfield picking up her needles and resuming her work where she'd left off before the interruption.

Xavier rushed through the kitchen and out the back door, being careful once again not to let the screen door slam. He waited at the wagon until he saw Oggie coming through the hedges that separated the Bartholomew and Winfield properties. Xavier looked closely at Oggie's face and judging from his expression suspected trouble.

"Everything all right Og?" Asked he of his friend.

"Yeah buddy," Oggie responded with glee. "Except I'm not sure my mom really knows that I'm leavin'."

"What da' ya mean," asked Xavier.

"Well, she was on the phone in one of those whispering conversations and she wouldn't hardly talk to me. When she did, I told her 'me an' Xavier are leavin' mom,' all she did was put her finger to her mouth and said, 'shhh.' Then she gave me a kiss on the cheek and whispered, 'see ya' later hon,' so, what'da ya think Xav?"

"She said 'see ya' right?"

"Sure, but--"

"An' she knew before that you were goin' right?"

"Well yeah, but---"

"So, let's get goin' before they change their minds; and, maybe we can get camp set up before noon."

"O.K. Xav. Let's go!"

CHAPTER 8

THE HIKE

It took the boys about two hours to get through their small town pushing and pulling that heavy heaping overloaded wagon. Just about everyone they passed wanted to know what the boys were doing with the loaded wagon. And of course, they gave everyone a short descriptive report of their expedition plans.

Leaving town, the old Winfield Farm was about a half mile north on state route 95. As the boys pushed and pulled the heavy, high heaped, wagon, Xavier noticed how the weeds had grown up in the center of the graveled lane that lead up past where the house used to be and the remains of the fallen barn.

"Wonder how the trail is going to be back on the hill?"

"What'da ya' mean?" Asked Oggie panting and nearly out of breath from pulling the wagon.

"Well, look at the weeds here in the yard."

"Oh yeah. Wow, hope it's not grown up like this."

When they reached the widened part of the drive, nearly beside where the large two-story house used to be, Oggie stopped pulling the wagon.

"Hey, let's take a break," Oggie pleaded, wiping the beads of sweat from his forehead.

"Phew! We must have packed everything. This wagon seems to be getting heavier," responded Xavier.

"I know Xav. Can we take a break?"

"Sure Og. Let's move over there under that big ol' tree."

Next to the foundation where the old farmhouse had been, stood a large oak tree that most likely had been there for twenty or thirty years judging from the size of it's trunk. The boys pushed the wagon up the remaining incline of the drive that they had been ascending for the last fifteen minutes or so. The house was not visible from the highway, making for a rather long driveway.

Plopping down on the ground, Oggie inquired of his comrade.

"Whew, maybe we ought to camp here, Xav?"

"Naw, we gotta go deep in the woods."

"But it's cleared here, an' there's shade and water at that ole well I'll bet."

"Sure there's water there, but this isn't wilderness. This is civilization. We wanna be in the wild, Og."

"But I'm tired man," continued Xav's heavier and out of energy counterpart.

"Come on pal, don't give up on me now, 'cause we're only half way there. An' the tough part is yet to come."

"What! What'da ya mean?" Oggie both exclaimed and also questioned.

"Well, up to now we've been in town on hard roads ya know?"

Oggie nodded his head in affirmation.

"Where the drive ends there's a trail that used to be a strip mine road and that's where we're going.

"Aw, you mean back where that big open place is like in 'Journey to the Center of the Earth? Where those cliffs are?"

"Yeah, that's the place."

"But if we went in the woods behind the high school like you and I used to, we'd be there by now Xav?" Pleaded the now weary and nearly worn out heavy weight.

"Do you think we could have pulled this loaded wagon along that narrow, rocky, cliff trail knucklehead?"

"Naw, I guess not."

"Well, that's why we came this way. An' anyway, we're not going there."

"What? I like that place. An' if we're not going there, then where are we going?"

"Well, this road here," Xavier stood up and pointed to the drive they had just come on from the highway, then continued, "goes there and enters the woods."

He moved around to the front of the wagon as he pointed to a spot at the end of the drive that only barely looked like a road because of the late June grass that had grown so high.

"And we'll follow that to a point where there's a hard left in the road that goes up to the *center of the earth* area." By *center of the earth* area the boys were referring to the Jules Verne novel, *Journey to the Center of the Earth* that was one of Xavier's favorite reads.

"Yeah?" Inquired Oggie, squinting his face and shaking his head back and forth quickly.

"Well that's not where we're goin..."

Before Xavier could finish, Oggie interrupted, "how come?"

"Well, at that sharp left, after a little brick dynamite house, there's an older hidden road to the right..."

Oggie again interrupted, this time with excitement, "a dynamite house?"

"Yea, it is just off the road a little."

"Is there dynamite in it?"

"There used to be. I know 'cause my dad told me so."

"Hey let's go check it out!"

"I don't think there's any in it anymore," said Xavier trying to calm his friend, since he knew that there was no dynamite there anymore.

"Ya never know, Xav. They might have left a stick in there."

"I don't think they'd be so careless. An' anyway you'd need a cap to set it off."

"Huh?" Oggie questioned, dimpling his forehead and shrugging his upper lip.

"Dynamite needs a dynamite cap to set it off."

"Naw," said Oggie, "I think you can just throw it and it'll blow up. I've seen cowboys do it on TV."

"You mean you've seen 'em light it and throw it."

"Yeah. But we got matches!" Popped back Oggie excitedly.

"Look Oggie, that's powder cap dynamite."

"Huh?"

"Dynamite needs a little explosion to set it off." Oggie turned his head with a questioning look as he gave Xavier all his attention for this lesson.

"That's what a dynamite cap is. It's a little explosion like a fire cracker that sets off the dynamite." Xavier continued.

Tilting his head to the other side, Oggie continued inquisitively with a serious inquiry.

"You sure, Xav?"

"Yep, I read it in a book about Alfred Nobel."

"Who's he?"

"The guy that invented nitro glycerin."

Oggie seemed to be digesting what Xavier had told him so far.

"I thought we were talking about dynamite. What's nitro glycerin got to do with dynamite?"

"It's nitro glycerin and that's what's in dynamite."

"This is interesting," Oggie said nodding his head in affirmation that he was beginning to understand then continuing, " I mean, really?"

"Really!" Responded Xavier nodding his head in affirmation, "I read all about it in this book about Nobel and his inventions an' his life. He made nitro glycerin first and it exploded too easy. Just shaking the nitro, it would go off."

"Really?" Oggie's lip dropped in amazement.

"Yep. One of Nobel's family members was killed when one of the bottles of liquid nitro leaked down into the wagon wheel where it was hooked to the wagon an' it blew up and killed a bunch of people."

"Wow!" Oggie was dancing with excitement.

"Then Nobel *experimented* how to make it safe. He found that the nitro was safe when it was absorbed in a mixture of sawdust and some kind of clay material I think. It wouldn't blow up then. In fact, you could hit it with a hammer; a big hammer like a sledge and it wouldn't blow up."

"Well, that's no good," said Oggie.

"Sure it is. That way it can be produced and carried around safely. You know, like to our hardware store."

"You mean our hardware store has some?"

"I think so."

"What's that stuff called again?"

"In the sawdust and clay, or the liquid?" Asked Xavier wanting to clarify Oggie's question.

"The stuff that you can carry around."

"That's dynamite."

"You mean...?"

"Dynamite is the safe version of nitro glycerin. It needs a little explosion to set it off and then it really blows stuff up."

Oggie was excited. "Let's go an' see if there's any left in that dynamite house!"

"I'm tellin' ya' man, that I don't think there is any left there."

Oggie pressed on.

"Let's go see!" Oggie turned and started for the road trail.

Xavier knelt down to push the wagon and doing so noticed that his friend was walking away.

"Where ya goin' Og?"

Oggie stopped and turned around.

"To go see that dynamite house."

Xavier stood still, propped his arms on his hips and with a scowl on his face, perked to his excited friend.

"Well, don't ya' think that we oughta take the wagon brainless!"

"Oh yeah. Sorry man. I just wanna see that dynamite house real bad."

Oggie came back and the boys traded positions with Oggie pushing the wagon and Xavier pulling and leading the way.

CHAPTER 9

ROUGH GOING

Continuing steadily upward since the exit from the hard surface State Highway 95 and now moving deeper into the woods, on their left were tall banks of sandy loam, clay, and small stones, giving evidence of a much earlier strip mining from years ago in this part of the trail, and although mostly grown up with vegetation now, the path was still mostly a graveled roadbed and was peppered with sparsely populated tall grass about knee high with an occasional stem standing waist high. On the right the woods appeared to be undisturbed.

The boys continued up this slightly rutted roadbed, pressing deeper into the woods, pushing and shoving the loaded wagon onward until all at once without warning, Oggie stopped pushing and stood up.

"Hey, this pushins' harder."

Nearly dislocating his arms when the wagons weight exceeded his ability to pull when Oggie stopped pushing, Xavier became upset.

"Tell me about it Lardo!" He shouted.

"Hey watch it man," Oggie pouted back in a testy fashion.

"Who do ya think has been pushin' for the last two hours peanut brain?"

"Why didn't ya tell me," Oggie demanded.

"Cause I'm not a complainer; just a doer."

"Hey, I'm a doer too," said Oggie.

"Well, we don't seem to be doin' much right this minute," Xavier explained lifting his hands chest high with his palms pointed upward and fingers stretched outward indicating a 'what now' expression.

"O.K. man, let's go," said Oggie leaning forward placing both hands on the upper part of the high load of the wagon. Xavier turned and started to tug on the tongue of the wagon noticing that the load seemed heavier than before. He reasoned that either the oil that he and Oggie had squirted on the wheels and axle had evaporated from friction heat because of the weight of the load, or that they were getting more tired and the load only seemed heavier. Either way, Xavier mentally concluded that they should continue without any further stops or delays.

"Hey Xav?" Panted Oggie.

"What now?" Frowned Xavier fully expecting yet another stop.

"You were tellin'," he gave another gasping pant, "about where we're goin' ta camp."

He panted several times more before continuing, "So, what about it?"

"Oh yeah. After the dynamite house a little ways there's this old mining road leading up to an abandoned strip mine that's real old. I think it was like the first mine here on great grandpa's farm. The road's hard to find but I remember because of the dynamite house. Ya' know?" After each sentence Xavier too panted, but not nearly as much as his short winded counterpart, who being overweight, had excess baggage to carry even before pushing or pulling on a wagon.

"Yea," Oggie responded even though he actually had no idea of where the road was. It was just two young boys way of acknowledging that they were plugged in and understanding each other clearly thus far.

"Well, you'll like it Og, it's got a real big pond an' we used to swim there before dad got this job that's makes him gone all the time." For a split second Xavier recalled when he and his dad Theodore would come here often and swim on hot summer days, that is, before his dad took that traveling sales job for the Pine Hill Clay Company. 'Yes, those were the days,' he thought, when the family would come to visit *great* grandpa and grandma Winfield and he and his dad, maybe even grandpa Winfield, would slip off in the woods and take quick dip in the cool water of the woods pond. Since his dad had taken the Pine Hill Clay sales job though, he was on the road traveling most of the week and then playing catch up around the house on chores, repairs, or building the addition after Natalie was born, and thus there just hadn't been much family time anymore. For just a moment, even a few seconds, Xavier felt saddened, wished his dad and mom were home, even missed his sister Natty; however, those fleeting thoughts were interrupted and quickly disposed.

"A pond? Is it deep?" Oggie's eyes lit up again.

"I don't remember. Haven't been there for a long time. Great grandpa took my dad and I there when I was a lot younger.

"Wow, let's get goin!" Oggie leaned against the load and started pushing with a new *zeal*. Xavier responded by two stepping forward to catch up with Oggie's lunge of excitement.

The boys snaked the wagon up the ever winding inclined path remaining in the gravel based grown up roadway that worked it's way deeper and deeper into the woods. The pathway was the remainder of the old roadbed that carried large construction vehicles and trucks extracting coal when Chestnut Ridge was a booming mining town some 10-20 years ago. With time, the local coal mining industry had declined from being the regions only major industry to a mere small lone mine far from town now. Earlier mining was crude with older steam powered shovels and small six wheeled dump trucks by comparison to today's mining that is accomplished with the use of advanced excavation conveyors and large dozers and multi-axle trucks.

Furthermore, early surface mining destroyed most of the ground surface top soil, leaving a sandy clay exposed where the mining companies left the work 'as is' with large crevices and poor soil fertility, leaving it thusly poor in supporting plant life outside a few locust and pine trees. Moreover, while the land was rendered useless for commercial reasons, it was quite a discovery zone for a couple of young boys like Xavier and Oggie. By comparison however, today's law requires that surface miners reclaim the ground and plant vegetation once the mining operation is completed, thus rendering the stripped area usable.

After about another hour of tugging, pushing, and stopping for the occasional rest and chat, the boys were within eyesight of the large bend in the road, which Xavier knew to be near the old dynamite house. They had just stopped the wagon after a long distance push up a much steeper incline portion of the path, to an almost level stretch which revealed the sharp bend to the left and a marked change in the terrain.

"It's somewhere around here Oggie." Xavier said panting for breath and wiping his forehead with a bright red handkerchief having a white patch pattern on it.

"Where?" Oggie inquired leaning on the wagon heap and looking around in the woods along the path ahead.

"Let's see," said Xavier dropping the wagon tongue and proceeding up the path a short ways ahead.

"As I remember, the dynamite house was on the right side of the road here somewhere. It's got a metal roof, but boy is this place grown up. When Gramps brought me up here the last time this was all cleared along the sides of the roads."

"Look!" Hollered Xavier as he ran into the brush on the left side of the path and road, to the edge, where there was the remains of a deep drainage ditch.

"What is it?" Exclaimed Oggie, taking off in a sprint after Xavier.

Xavier disappeared in the under brush while Oggie ran around the wagon and headed to the spot where his explorer friend had jumped into the ditch and disappeared. From this point, Oggie could see what the excitement was. Berries. Blackberries.

"Wow! Look at 'em, Og!"

"Yeah man! Is this great or what?"

"Eat up, Og."

"Are they O.K. like this? I mean do they need to be washed or wiped off or something?"

Xavier took about six or seven and popped them in his mouth.

"Those ones at the store are sprayed with stuff. These are in the raw, they're fresh and undefiled by mankind."

"You sure, Xav?"

"Sure. Gramps and I used to eat 'em every time we came up here. I forgot about 'em. Eat up, they're great."

"O.K., but I sure hope they won't hurt us," piped back Oggie. Even though he trusted his smarter friend, he still concerned himself with whether or not Xavier really knew for sure, or was just acting like he knew. For, there were times when Xavier acted like the expert, but actually was a total novice. Like the time when he and Oggie got the brainstorm to make homemade ice cream and got sick because the recipe they used turned out not to be home made ice cream at all, but a cake that required baking, in which Xavier's mother had written the words 'homemade ice cream' at the top of the recipe card so she would remember that this cake was especially good with home made ice cream. He pondered, if this situation were similar. Were these berries really safe? 'Oh well,' he thought, 'Xavier was exceptionally smart and obviously believed that the berries were safe judging from the way in which he was consuming them. And thus,' Oggie reasoned, while popping off a few lush and ripe blackberries, 'I sure am hungry,' then looked at them for two seconds and stuffed them in his mouth reaching for more.

"Wow, these are good."

"Told ya man. Look how big they are here along the bank."

Oggie stepped through the dried up drainage ditch and attempted to climb up the loose clay bank to where his friend was. Slipping a few times, he eventually conquered the climb and after dusting off, was quickly consuming berries with two nearly chubby but stout little hands.

The boys followed the berry patch along the *excavation* side of the roadway, inching their way further up the inclined road path, consuming berries every step of the way. Occasionally, they would look back to check their position with the road and wagon. As they began to reach their fill, they also reached an embankment preventing further conveyance alongside the road. It was a grown up cut in the bank from erosion and vegetation.

"Hey, look there's a stream of water coming out of the bank here," said Xavier kneeling to the ground on his knees.

Oggie left the berry patch and moved behind his best friend.

"It's a spring, Xav."

"Yea. I don't know about you, but I'm thirsty."

Oggie had a puzzled look, "you're not gonna drink that are ya?"

"Sure, what else would you expect an explorer to do? We're eating off the land, why not drink of the nectar of the earth."

And with that, Xavier cupped his hands together catching water from where the water ran out of the hillside over a rock, using the water to rinse off his hands.

"It's cold, Og. Nice and cold."

Xavier then cupped his hands together, held them under the small waterfall with a stream about the size of a trickling garden hose, and proceeded to get a drink by slurping up the wetness from the pool in his hands first.

"Think its O.K.?"

"Sure, we can see where it's coming from under that big rock right there," pointing to a large boulder up hill from them.

"An' there's nothing to get in it from there to where we are. Only water out in nature that you can't tell where it's coming from is questionable. Yep, we got a source of clean, cool, water here, Og."

Balanced between the wall of the embankment and the ledge of the drainage ditch, the boys held onto each other and traded paces supporting themselves on an eroded sand and clay embankment by punching their feet into the clay and sand, in this vertical ravine produced by the eroding run of the spring water.

While Oggie got his drink, Xavier surveyed their journey visually from the wagon back, then forward up the trail ahead of the wagon. While continuing his gaze up the trail ahead of the wagon, the bank had inclined at a steeper rate than the road, and they were now about 20 feet elevation above the road having climbed there without noticing the ascension of their climb.

"Man what a view," exclaimed Xavier. Oggie maneuvered himself to a standing position nearly causing Xavier to loose his footing on the ledge of the drainage ditch erosion.

"You got mud on your knees klutz," Xavier said pointing to Oggie's muddy wet pants.

"How'd you do it, Xav?"

"I squatted with my knees bending and spread so as not to get muddy."

"Oh!"

Oggie looked around intently and studied the area.

"Hey wouldn't it be neat to feel like maybe we're the first persons ever to be here?" He asked.

"Yeah. I don't hear any cars or any town or factory sounds any more. Listen." It was statement as much as a question.

The boys listened intently. The only audible sounds were those of an occasional twig scratching another, or something falling from a tree that had been loosened from the light wind, and of course the wind that was moving only the uppermost treetops of the highest trees. Otherwise, It was almost total quiet. Pondering their *serenity*, they sat on the ledge of the drainage ditch ledge for probably 10 or 15 minutes, maybe even a half an hour; it was so serene here. Occasionally they would scratch loose some of the clay surface of the drainage ditch wall with their high top tennis shoes as they dangled their legs down over the side wall. The loosened particles would trickle down the mildly inclined wall much like a boulder would wander down a hillside.

For a moment, or even several moments, Oggie imagined this wall was a large mountain cliff in Colorado or Montana, and that he was gazing at this large mountain from afar, wherein the loosened pieces were large boulders that bounced and rolled violently down the side of the mountain to crash on the ground below producing a small dust cloud that was sure to terrify residents in the local imaginary cites and towns in this make believe scene in his mind. Moreover, not knowing so, both he and Xavier were daydreaming similar boulder experiences, although Xavier's was much more vivid and grandeur. However, silence and daydream had to be broken.

"Man is this great or what?" Said Oggie waving his hands to indicate the vastness of their surroundings.

"Yeah," Xavier replied, studying the terrain of the road.

"Imagine what the Indians felt like when they were here and them knowing that no one had ever been here before."

"Yeah," said Xavier looking intently into the woods up hill to the left and across the road from where they were.

"It's like we're Indians and we're the first here," continued the firm little dreamer. Oggie looked around and actually felt like an explorer and imagined they were there for the first time. Actually, he was here in these particular woods for the first time.

"It's like we're settling the land. I mean we are going to settle a campsite, right?"

"Uh-huh," responded Xavier slowly and casually as though he were lost in a daydream. Xavier was looking more intently than before, now at one spot in particular near a clump of piled clay and rock along the far side of the roadbed.

Noticing the incoherent voice of his pal, and now observing the intensity of his best buddies study of a particular spot, Oggie squinted his eyes to focus on the same area.

"What is it?" He inquired.

"I don't know." Xavier pointed to the exact spot where he was investigating.

"Over there just beyond that large pile of dirt." He continued.

"I don't see anything, Xav."

"I can't tell what it is, Og."

Just then there was a muffled sound of metal clanging where Xavier was staring. Xavier carefully managed to pull his feet up and stand erect, then pointed to the right of the clay pile and screamed out.

"LOOK! OVER THERE!"

CHAPTER 10

EUREKA

Oggie jumped up quickly, grabbing hold of Xavier for stability, which nearly caused the two of them to lose their balance, and then tip toed to see what Xavier was pointing to occasionally catching glimpses of what looked like a metal roofed building.

"It's it, Og."

Oggie stretched to see, then gasped to catch his breath.

"For crying out loud Xav, you scared me half to death!"

"Sorry Og. But, I knew it had to be there somewhere."

Oggie leaned forward and breathed in deeply a couple times.

"You O.K., Og?"

"You scared me man! I thought it was something bad."

"Naw, it's just the dynamite shed. Something must've popped on the roof or something. You know like the metal expanding from the heat of the sun or something."

"Sure Xav, but don't ever do that again."

"Sorry Og, I didn't think. I just knew it was there and got excited when I found it." Xavier looked at the angled bank below them and pondered how to get down without having to go all the way back through the berries. He then looked back over toward the shed and pointed just up the road to the left of the little building.

"See that clump of dirt, Og?"

"Yeah," responded Oggie looking to where Xavier was pointing.

"Look back in the woods between the dynamite shed and the bend in the road. What'da ya see?"

"Trees."

"Naw. Look at the ground."

Oggie squinted and pushed his visual depth perception as far as he could.

"Look's like another road. But, it's all grown up."

"Yep, that's our road to the pond where we're gonna camp."

"Cool, Xav. But that's gonna be tough gettin' the wagon up through there."

"Yeah, but we don't have far to go up through there. It's just over that hill," said Xavier pointing into the woods to an observable hillcrest.

"Reckon we wouldn't have found that road if we hadn't got in these berries and came up here." Xavier pointed out.

Oggie surveyed the road and the hidden entrance to the older road they were talking about.

You got that right, Xav. We're lucky."

"Naw, we planned it that way." They both looked at each other and laughed.

"Come on Og, let's go." And with that, Xavier sat down on the ledge of the drainage ditch bank, jerked his legs and butt forward, slid off the edge of the ledge, and slid down the side of the clay and sandy like surface on his rump.

"Ahhh!" screamed Xavier as he rapidly slid down the walled ravine leaving a dust trail behind him. When he hit bottom he bounced on his feet and plunged forward to avoid gettin' the falling debris down his back that trailed behind him.

"Wow, was that cool!" Exclaimed Xavier brushing the rear of his pants.

"Yer nuts Xavier Winfield!" hollered Oggie down to his dust-covered friend.

"Come on man, you can do it," pleaded Xavier motioning for Oggie to slide down the hill.

"No way man; I'll get killed!"

"No you won't. Just time it so that when you're feet hit the bottom that you spring your legs to take the shock and then jump forward like I did."

"But I'll break a leg or something," Oggie rebounded.

"Naw," snapped back Xavier, "just do like I said and you'll be O.K."

Not wanting Xavier to think he was chicken, Oggie sat down and jerked his body stiff and hollered, "O.K., here goes!"

The rounder of the two slid down the side of the drainage ditch bank gracefully but not so graceful in his stop. He stopped abruptly with a cloud of clay and dust settling on top of the lifeless figure in the ditch.

"You O.K., Oggie?" Xavier inquired running over to see the outcome of his buddy, "man you sure made a lot of dust; that was cool."

"Yeah. Well, maybe I'm dead." Responded Oggie with his eyes closed and the dust and clay gravel still trickling off his back as he coughed a couple times rolling on this side then getting up on his knees.

Xavier jumped into the ditch. "Close your eyes man, you got dust all in your hair and all over your back."

Oggie closed his eyes while Xavier shook his fingers through Oggie's hair, followed by patting Oggie's back and brushing his front.

"Let's go, Og."

"O.K. man, let's check it out." Xavier turned in the direction of the building and took off.

The boys ran to the area where they observed the shed, and sure enough, hidden in the growth, there it was. Made of concrete block with an angled metal roof that pitched downward from front to back, the dynamite shed it surely was. For, even though nearly worn away by the years of sun and weather fading, the letters D Y N A M I T E were still barely visible printed on the partly opened door.

"Look, the doors open," said Oggie, "I hope there's at least one stick left. Wow!"

"I doubt it Og, with the door being open?"

"You never know Xav."

"Yeah you're right. But, let's check it out anyway."

The boys waded down through the high grass and sticky briars to the slightly open large metal door. Peeking inside, the boys were almost on top of each other holding tightly to each other's tee shirt with a pinch. The inside was lighted some with the cracked open door, and also by a beam of light from a back corner of the building where a piece of the roof's sheet metal roof had been peeled back. Apparently someone had forced the roofing back to see inside, perhaps during the shed's last days of service before the lock had been removed they reasoned.

"Step inside Xav."

"No way Og," said Xavier stepping back a step, "you."

"I'll follow you if you go ahead."

"You're chicken to go first," Xavier tempted.

"I'm not chicken, it's just you're older and bigger. An', yer smarter too, just in case."

"In case what?"

"I don't know? Just in case."

Suddenly, Xavier swiftly disappeared through the open door with a flash as if he had been jerked inside scaring Oggie half out of his wits. Oggie jumped back about five feet or so and screamed, "Xavier! Xavier! Come out!"

Inside the building Oggie heard banging against the door and his best friend screaming.

"Let me go! Help! Oggie! Help!"

Frantically, Oggie paced his feet left and right, back and forth, in excitement trying to decide what to do. 'How could he help?' he thought. 'He was too small to help. What could he do?'

"Help!" The screams continued, with the continued loud clanging.

Oggie figured he should at least try to save his life long buddy. He hesitantly moved over to the clanging door.

"I'm comin' in Xav," to which, he stamped his feet loudly as he started through the metal door with his eyes squinted half closed, screaming loudly as he proceeded.

"HERE I COME!"

Arms grabbed him immediately at his chest and then at his neck. He squinted his eyes closed and swung his arms frantically, connecting with nothing. His eyes were glued closed, for he couldn't stand the thought to look; to see; what awfulness had attacked and apparently consumed his best friend. For, he no longer heard the voice of Xavier. He grabbed the arms that had hold of him, and they were human. A boys arms as it were. He dared a glimpse to see. Cracking open his eye, to his amazement, Xavier was alive and he was directly in front. It was Xavier's arms outstretched in front of him, which Oggie was hanging on to.

"You are a horses rear!" screamed Oggie. Xavier sprang from the door a few steps, and out of arms reach of Oggie as he burst into laughter. It was that kind of laughter that comes from deep down in one's stomach that continues loud and frantically without control.

"You are a real rear end, Xavier!" exclaimed Oggie straightening up his shirt and tucking the tail of his tee shirt into his trousers.

"I mean a total horses rear!" Oggie was very upset.

"You. . . .you should've. . . . .you should've seen your face," hollered Xavier with laughter that just got more intense and less controllable as Xavier continued, his conversation being broken by bursts of intense laughter.

"I mean…., it was hilarious."

"Yeah. Laugh! At my expense your havin' a ball." Asserted Oggie.

"Just remember every dog has its day, Xav."

No sooner had Oggie said this than Xavier tripped on a rock while stomping in the tall weeds and briars and passionately laughing. The fall caused him to fall into a mess of sharp briars.

"OW!" Hollered Xavier.

"Oh, shut up."

"Your eyes got as big as saucers, Og." Shouted Xavier through laughter as he tugged carefully at briars with two fingers pinching briar stems to disconnect them from his clothes.

The laughing was catching. Oggie thought about what Xavier had said and then compared that to what he had been thinking, and soon he too was engrossed in laughter. It started with a chuckle, and then intensified into a roar.

"I bet I looked like something," then surging with a belly laugh Oggie shook like a firm bowl of *gelatin*.

"Was it bad or what?" He added.

"It was bad, Oggie. You'll have to owe me for that. It was great."

The two boys laughed at each other for what seemed like ten or fifteen minutes, still just outside the shed at the door threshold.

"Oh; oh," hiccupped Xavier, "my stomach hurts."

"Mine too," returned Oggie.

"I. . .I can't. . . . Stand it, (hic). It. . . it hurts (hic)!" Continued Xavier as he maneuvered the rest of the way out the barely opened door, following Oggie, who had already, exited the dark, damp, dingy, shed.

Xavier tripped at the doorframe and fell into the back of Oggie, causing the two of them to land on the ground abruptly, with Xavier rolling over top Oggie, while the two of them continued struggling to regain self control over their frantic unrestrained laughing.

Oggie was on his knees in front of the door holding his face with both hands to quench his hurting facial muscles from the intensity of the laughter. Xavier sat up from his lying position in the briars and wiped the tears from his eyes and cheeks, then using his T shirt, he cleaned his gold rimmed glasses and aimed them to the sky to see that the lenses were clean. Finally, only an occasional chuckle remained now and then in between his comical hiccupping. He lowered his glasses onto his head adjusting their position for maximum comfort, while Oggie was still on his knees at the doorway.

"You were great, Oggie (hic)."

"You weren't bad yourself, Xav."

Oggie was stretching his facial muscles by pushing his hands against his face in an attempt to get rid of the face cramps. Xavier started to get up from the briars and instantly stopped abruptly and looked over Oggie's head.

"Ahhh!!" screamed Xavier reaching out his hands and springing his body forward on the ground toward Oggie.

"AAhhhhhhhh!" Startled at first then guessing this was Xavier's way to overcome the laughter, Oggie started laughing again and fought back against Xavier's reaching arms as before. Xavier grabbed at Oggie again and again, grasping at Oggie's tee shirt, and tugging at him violently to come toward the road.

"Your nuts Xav. You break me up." Xavier spoke nothing, in fact it was as though he could not speak, as if he were totally distracted, and just kept *vehemently* jerking on Oggie's tee shirt. Oggie noticed his facial expression. It was not an anxious expression as when one is kidding but one of fear, and his eyes were focused above Oggie's head. Oggie stopped resisting the tugs of his friend for a split second to fall for the pun and glanced behind and overhead him where Xavier's eyes seemed fixed. Oggie's glance was just for a split second because he knew not whether Xavier could be trusted. His heart nearly stopped, for dangling from the roof of the building downward to about 3 or 4 feet from his head and waving to and fro in no particular pattern was a large snake measuring about 3 inches in diameter.

"Ahhhhh! Ahhhhh!!" screamed Oggie looking over his shoulders and pushing forward at Xavier frantically to get away, ultimately pushing Xaiver over and onto the ground as both boys fell and scrambled ferociously to get up. The snake was loosing its' hold and appearing to be coming to the ground. Oggie jerked his feet violently trying to get clear of the dropping intruder that measured some 6 or 7 feet long.

"It's comin' after me!" screamed Oggie awkwardly grasping for Xavier's legs that were also feverishly scrambling to incline the small bank that had lead them down to the shed from the roadbed. Suddenly, with a thud, the snake fell to the ground. Both boys screamed and fought to get away.

"Ahhhhhhh! Help!" screamed Oggie finally getting a foothold and lunging forward over Xavier's right side. He ran through the briars that tore feverishly at his clothing and skin. He felt the cuts go deep in his arms, concerned only for the moment about how the briars tugged at him and delayed his escape. Xavier too, got control of his footing and followed Oggie's footsteps experiencing the same excruciating cuts and tearing at his arms and sides.

Safely in the roadway, the boys were bent over with their hands on their knees supporting their upper bodies as they swayed slightly back and forth, breathing heavily and deeply, trying to catch their breath and shake the creepy feeling off their skin of the possibility of being bitten by a snake seconds past. Oggie expelled his berry picking all over the ground following a sudden knot that had developed in his stomach in between nearly crying and almost passing out. In the distance, they could hear the rustle of the weeds as their intruder snaked its' way into the woods uphill in the direction of the hidden roadway.

"That was too close!" gasped Xavier.

"Yer not kiddin'," panted Oggie, "I thought we were goners!"

"Me too!" exclaimed Xavier. Xavier started stomping his feet and shuddering all over.

"What is it Xav?"

"Ahhhhhhh! Screamed Xavier his whole body shaking then shouting loudly. "I was in that building when it was overhead me!"

Both boys shook violently and their skin crawled. Wanting to shake the awfulness that slithered on the surface of their skin, they brushed their arms as if the intruder had somehow gotten hold of them or had somehow left traces of his intrusion on the surface of their bodies.

"That was scary!"

"You're not kidding!"

"You know I'm not, Og."

"I know Xav, it's just awful to think how close we came to death."

Regaining some of his composure and color, Xavier asked, as if directed to no one in particular, "Wonder what kind of snake it was?"

"Who cares," answered Oggie.

"I do, I'll bet it was only a black snake."

"It was big! I mean real big!"

"It was at that, Oggie. But, I'll bet it wasn't poisonous. We probably weren't in any danger at all."

"It's all right. We're not in any danger now and we don't have to know what kind of snake it was to still be safe."

"Let's check it out Og," said Xavier slowly walking toward the building as if to be urging his frightened friend to come along.

"Go ahead Xav. But, I'll pass."

Xavier looked intently in the direction of the upper side of the hill where the sounds of the departing intruder had dissipated. But, nowhere was there a view of a snake. Xavier really didn't desire to venture further, but he did want Oggie to at least think he did.

"Come on, Og," said he rustling the edge of the high brush.

"Like I said Xav, go ahead. I'll be waiting at the wagon after ya' find it and get bit. Oh and remember . . . we got a snake bite kit; so, I'll treat ya."

"Oh, all right," replied Xavier with a disgusting voice, turning back toward his friend, who had already begun returning downhill toward the wagon.

CHAPTER 11

THE POND

Back at the wagon, the boys treated their briar wounds and scratches with the First Aid Kit. There were many, and they used up several paper towels wetting the towels with water to wash the wounds and scratches clean, before treating them. They doused the wounds with Mercurochrome. When finished doctoring, Xavier and Oggie stuffed away the spent paper towels in between the anchored canteen and the tent so as not to leave a mess on the trail and also so they'd have some paper to burn once the towels dried.

Continuing the trail to adventure, Xavier lead them to the hidden side trail after some difficulty distinguishing exactly where the older long forgotten trail began. For one, when the new road had been cleared, the dozer had left a two-foot high hump in front of the older entrance, making it appear unnoticeable. Secondly, since this was where the new road made a sharp and steep turn to the left, there was a lot of dirt piled up where the bank had been excavated with a deep cut to clear the entrance gradually up hill leftward. To the left of that turn was the same bank that the boys earlier had been ascending while eating the berries. In fact, if one were to examine the area a little closer, they would discover that the older road made a slight bend to the right gradually inclining steeper and steeper with each forward step. And, since abandoned many years ago, the road itself now had small locust trees populating it, making the road not only nearly invisible, but also impassable by a motor vehicle.

At the transition point, they had to maneuver the wagon up and over the piled sand and clay at the road edge, and in doing so, they spilled some of the tied on load, and had to stop to repack on the other side of the hump. After repacking, when they returned to their pushing and pulling upward, they had not noticed that all their packed newspapers and wet paper towels from earlier had dislodged and fallen by the wayside. Moreover, the loss was permeated by the fact that they were somewhat distracted now, since this was the area where the snake from earlier had disappeared. The boys had made the transition and were now scaling the ever-increasing incline.

"Whew! This is tough, Xav. Let's stop."

Grunting and gasping, Xavier responded, "naw, (gasp) we only have (gasp) a little ways to go now."

"Yeah, but it's steep now." Oggie stopped pushing and unable to pull by himself, Xavier slipped on the clay surface falling on his rear. He lay there looking up through the well-leafed trees of summer. It was much cooler on this road in the shade than where they had been earlier in the sun. They were deep in heavy tree forestation that now offered cover from the hot afternoon heat. However, in the forest they could only see and hear the breeze that was gradually swaying the treetops although feeling none of it on their hot sweaty skin because of the hard work of moving Oggie's loaded wagon up the steeper incline of this part of the journey. On the newer road, it was open and they had been roasting in the sweltering sun. Now, however, their world appeared much different. It was as though no mining had been done here at all. The trees were large, the ground covered with the under brush of leaves and sticks from fallen tree branches, and only patches of visible clay on the very eroded, portions of roadbed that fortunately were infrequent.

"I don't think I'll make it, Xav," said Oggie lying down beside Xavier looking up through the trees while wiping droplets of sweat from his forehead.

"Just think what it was like for the Indians, or the settlers," challenged Xavier.

"Yeah. Bet they loved it."

"Imagine being here for the first time."

"Yeah, with no one around. No houses, trains, cars, or factories."

"Yeah," said Xavier squinting to see the clouds beyond and above the roof of the treetops.

"No running water, no stoves, no paved roads; just us and the woods; oh, and the trees, the leaves and the berries of course; plus the trails that we make for ourselves. Yeah Og, its gonna be just us and the earth. Real living. No moms and dads telling us what to do; nope; just making our own decisions and livin'. This is freedom!" Oggie was proud of his conclusions.

"Yeah, freedom," added Xavier. "Just think, living with nature and the animals, everyday. With the foxes, the raccoons, the bears, and even the snakes." The trees rustled from a wind gush.

Feeling uneasy with Xavier's latest comments, Oggie sat up and looked around, focusing on the ground area adjacent to where they were, then outward to ensure that their circle of safety was clear.

"What's up?" inquired Xavier setting up mimicking his friend.

"Nuttin'."

"What ya lookin' for?"

"Nothing, really."

"Tell me," said Xavier almost pleading.

"I was just thinkin' about how much further we have to go."

"Yer kiddin'?" asked Xavier.

"No, why?"

"You mean you wanna get goin'?"

"Yeah," popped Oggie, standing up as if ready to go.

"That's a first. You must have an incentive."

"You said there's a pond, right?" Inquired Oggie not wanting Xavier to know that he wished they were clear of this area where shortly ago they'd had the encounter with fear.

"Yeah."

"I'm hot and wantin' ta go swimin' . . . like . . . real bad!" Oggie looked around casually for that unlikable creature.

"Let's go!" Xavier jerked to attention, grabbed the wagon tongue handle, and the two were back tugging and pushing the wagon up the steep incline which was now a very rutted road bed. Also, the trail now cut through the steep hillside with an elevated hill on both sides, a sort of gateway if you will. While they moved ever so slowly now, visions danced in Oggie's head of nightfall. He had always been afraid of the dark. Now, they seemed so deep in the woods and far away from civilization that he wondered what tonight would be like. He hadn't wanted Xavier to know, and feared that he'd reveal his fear by his own actions. Oggie knew that if Xavier were to find out he'd rib and tease him about it forever. Xavier must not find out. The visions of fear suddenly left as sharp pains shot up his legs, being almost cramp like, and just as they were cresting the top of the steep hill that they had been ascending for the past half hour or so, maybe even an hour.

"Ow!" Oggie exclaimed falling against the load, which thrust the wagon over the top of the ridge of the incline. The quick forward movement of the wagon caused him to fall to the ground.

"Ow! Ow! Ow!" he exclaimed grabbing the backside of his left leg. It was a cramp; and, it felt like a really bad one. It really wasn't, but he sure thought so. Xavier ran around and rubbed the leg pulling up Oggie's loose pant leg. In a few minutes the pain subsided and all was well.

"You need to take in more water Og." Oggie nodded his head and rubbed his leg while Xavier turned his attention back to looking around through the woods focusing his attention deeper than the area near to them.

Suddenly, Xavier sprang to life and hurried forward of the wagon, over the remaining portion of this last mild inclined grade, to a landing that opened expansive to his right.

"Oggie, LOOK!"

CHAPTER 12

THE CAMPSITE

This area was far more immense and grandeur than Xavier had remembered. The steep cliff, on the right side, the cool clear large body of water at the base of the face of the cliff, and the open clay soil expanding outward from the pond across from the cliff. Near where Xavier stood, the pushed back topsoil had given way to germinating 4 to 6 foot locust and pine trees. Then to top off the experience, the entire area was surrounded with large oak, hickory, and maple trees. It was the perfect campsite. Hidden, expansive, with water, sunlight, shade, and, well, just everything an explorer and camper could want.

Turning back toward his approaching explorer mate, Xavier looked at the roadway carved through the hillside those many years ago. This place was just perfect and almost just as he remembered it.

"Wow! This is great, Xav," said Oggie pausing to take in the sight.

"Look at that cliff!"

"Wow, it's great! Can we climb it?" Asked Oggie as he gazed it up and down. Its vertical incline was probably 30 feet or so, nearly as high as an electric pole.

"Sure. We can even scale the little part of the cliff, right here, then walk along the edge to get above the water."

"Then we can jump, Xav!"

"I don't know Og, it might be slopped too much."

"Oh, yea . . . you're right . . . maybe. Let's go swimin'." Oggie ran to the pond that was crystal clear with just the slightest light green tint at the deepest point the difference in color representing depth, but even so, one could clearly see the bottom. There was no sign of life in the pond, and at the farthest end were about a dozen short cattails stalking upward, to finish off an absolute perfect camp setting.

"Let's set up the campsite first, Og."

At the edge of the pond, Oggie swished his hand in the pond, "ah, come on let's swim."

"But then we'll get all sweaty again when we set up the tent and camping gear."

"Oh yea, you're right."

"If we set up first, we'll get all hot and then we can cool off with a swim."

"O.K. Let's set up!"

The boys moved the wagon with a newfound zeal and quickly sat up the tent on the gradual incline of clay that was across from the cliff. This was the perfect spot, with the pond out in front of the tent and the woods behind them. Xavier had pointed out that the morning sun would warm their tent for an early start each day, and shade would cast over them at evening and would cool their tent for a good nights sleep.

They gathered some stones to make a campfire pit and using the small army shovel dug a small pit for the fire pit and also cleared the topsoil for the tent site, since the tent had no bottom. Also, they had packed an old canvas tarp that was given them by some guys at the local brick manufacturing plant who had seen the boys collecting pop bottles and upon inquiring of the boys purpose had learned that there was need of a tarp to lay down on the ground before setting their sleep gear inside to protect their gear from getting wet should there be rain.

After setting up, Oggie lit the kerosene lantern as Xavier had instructed to make sure it would work before nightfall. However, since the kerosene had sloshed all around during their nearly four-hour journey, the outside of the lantern had a film of kerosene and immediately swished completely in flames. It took a few minutes for them to extinguish the fire by covering the lantern with extra bedding cloth to smother out the flames.

"Well, now that that disaster is over, why shouldn't we swim; I'm sweatin'," said Oggie.

"Yeah, me too, Og. Let's do it."

Oggie rustled through his clothes in the tent.

"Boy that's dumb?"

"What?"

"I'm looking for my swimin' trunks and I didn't bring any."

"Me either," said Xavier, "we'll go in our underwear or skinny dip."

"No way!"

Xavier shed all his clothes except for his underwear laid his eyeglasses on top of his clothes and headed for the water.

"You're not going like that are you?" Questioned Oggie looking around into the woods.

"Sure. You see me don't you? I mean, who's gonna see?"

Oggie looked around into the woods again, upon the cliff, and in amongst the locust and pine trees near the far end of the pond, as he heard the splashing of the cool water under Xavier's feet and legs walking into the pond.

"What if someone's out there?" Queried Oggie motioning his arms around, indicating all the area that surrounded them.

"Yeah. What if they are?"

"Well, . . . what if?" Continued Oggie.

Xavier dove in and came up a few feet ahead.

"WOW, this is great!" He screamed out.

"Shoot man. What if someone comes?" He heard the splashing of the cool tantalizing waters as Xavier fell into a backstroke.

"Yeah Og. You let me know if anyone accidentally finds this spot on *my* great grandfather's farm, hidden miles back in the woods, and I'll be sure and get out. O.K.?"

"Poop! Your right," to which Oggie stripped down to his whites, tiptoed on the jagged strip mine clay rocks to the edge of the pond, stepping in ever so softly.

"Oooo, yuck! It's muddy and slimy."

"What'd ya' expect?"

"But it's oozing between my toes." Said Oggie, jumping out wiggling his feet in the water along the edge to get the mud off.

"Don't worry about it, it's just mud Og."

"How come it's not clear anymore," asked Oggie noticing that the water had turned all cloudy where Xavier had been and was also now.

"Because it's a clay mud bottom. You know like dirt. It'll clear back up when we get out."

Xavier was now near the middle where the water was level with his chest.

"Look down there where I haven't been yet," pointing north toward the cattails.

"And there," Xavier shouted pointing toward the end where the road entrance was. Both ends were still crystal clear. He dove in and came up brushing water from his hair.

"Wow does this feel great!" He shouted with a refreshing voice.

"Oh yeah, I see," said Oggie looking at both ends and edging back in the water.

"Yuck! I don't know that I'll ever get used to this." Oggie squinted his eyes at the thought of slimy mud running between his toes and quickly dove forward coming up only a few yards from where Xavier stood.

"Quit complaining!" Shouted Xavier. Oggie's eyes suddenly opened wide.

"What if there's something in the water?" He asked.

"Like what?"

"You know; fish; snakes?"

Xavier laughed, "Did you see any when the water was crystal clear?" He waved his arms and hands about the pond.

"No. And besides, if there was anything in the water, they would be just as afraid of you as you are of them and would stay away."

Oggie nodded his head and frowned in affirmation but still kept on the alert near the cattails just in case Xavier was wrong. Although, in minutes he totally forgot about the contents of the water and along with Xavier, was swimming, cooling off, and skipping flat clay stones across the pond from one end to the other, pretending that the stones were boats and airplanes landing on a lake.

Having such a grand time, the boys hadn't noticed that many hours had passed since their arrival. After their four-hour journey there, and now nearly four and a half hours of in water and out of water fun including climbing part way up the inclined cliff and jumping in the water, it was nearly 7:00 p.m. Behind the tent the tall trees were beginning to cast a shadow on the ground in the direction of their tent.

Oggie suddenly became aware of his Superman wristwatch; a watch that he had received two years earlier on his eighth birthday.

"Oh man!"

"What?" Inquired Xavier.

"I forgot to take my watch off an' it's full'o water."

"Stupid! Why'd ya do that?"

"I didn't think."

"You never think."

"Stop it," demanded Oggie.

"What?" Then again, Xavier repeated, "What?"

"That's what my mom always says an' I don't like it."

"Well, she's right. You don't use your head, Og."

"Well, I wanted to get in the water like you did."

"No you didn't."

"I did too!"

"Then why all the hesitation? It's too muddy and there might be fish or snakes," mocked Xaiver, "Oh yeah, and it's oozing between my toes."

Oggie pushed Xavier backward and both boys fell in the water along the edge getting mud all over their sides and legs. They splashed water in each other's faces for another half hour when Oggie complained that Xavier wasn't playing fair. The shadows were now covering the tent leaving only the front top gable lighted and stretching to the waters edge.

"Hey Xav, it's starting to get dark."

"Yeah it is," said Xavier acting almost surprised. "We better get something to eat. Let's collect branches and twigs to make a fire."

CHAPTER 13

WHERE'S XAVIER?

The boys slipped their overalls on over their wet soaked underwear and their high top tennis shoes over their wet feet. Then, they collected twigs and fallen tree branches from the edge of the woods behind the tent. Behind the tent, the ground was flat for a short distance then dropped steeply for a distance of about sixty feet into the woods, so they tried to stay closer to the tent area. Because of the impending nightfall the boys could not see how far the woods continued away from the pond behind them, although in the distance they could barely see the crest of a hill where beyond the crest it was already dark which Xavier supposed was the cliff area he and his grandfather had gone to one time looking for deer tracks.

Xavier had instructed Oggie on the size of branches to collect and to layer the branches in the rock pit to get a good fire started.

"First crumple the paper we brought and put that on the bottom, then place smaller twigs and other burnable stuff on top of that. Then finally, these bigger ones go on top so that they dry out and get lots of heat as the flames go up through them so that they light. So, when that's all assembled, light the paper and nature will take care of the rest."

"We didn't bring paper did we?" Asked Oggie looking through the bags and pile of camping gear.

"Sure did. I packed it myself."

"Well, when we were unpacking the wagon, I don't remember seein' any."

"You sure?" Asked Xavier dropping the branch he was trying to break by holding the branch with one hand and stomping on it in the middle to break it.

Oggie continued breaking twigs and branches while Xavier searched high and low through their belongings for the paper. To assist because of the poor lighting now, Xavier used the flashlight to find and then light the kerosene lantern, now that it had finally dried out enough that it would not engulf in flames.

"I know I packed it on the wagon; I remember. But it sure isn't here now. Bet it fell off when the wagon load dumped this afternoon."

"May be," said Oggie with a worried look. "What'll we do now?"

"I'll get some leaves and brush from the woods."

Xavier took the flashlight and disappeared into the edge of the woods. After a very short time span, Oggie became aware of his loneliness at the campsite, especially when he heard a rustle of brush in the woods.

"Xavier!" Hollered Oggie. There was no answer.

"That you Xavier?" He asked; still no answer.

"Xavier!" Shouted Oggie again; only louder this time.

"Xavier! Where are you?" He shouted again this time cupping his hands together at his mouth to produce a megaphone effect to drive his voice further. Still there was no answer. Oggie stopped breaking sticks, picked up the lantern and headed to the edge of the woods stopping about 10 feet short of the darkened cover of the heavy foliage of the huge standing trees of this more mature portion of the woods.

"XXXAAVVIEEERRR!" He shouted with an elongation to each syllable. It was a method his mother often used when calling him to supper. Right now his thought of his mother flashed in his mind; wondering what she was doing right now. Pangs of hunger purged through him. If he were home, he'd have eaten by now and he'd be in the house. Safe.

He glanced at the sky that was now turning a medium dark sea blue with an almost orange cast near what little horizon that could be visible. There even appeared to be a couple lights in the heaven. However, under this thick overhead forest cover, the sky was barely visible and the darkness was now around everywhere making visibility nearly impossible without the lantern.

"XaavviieerrrRR!" He again hollered with emphasis at the end as though he were commanding a response. He held the lantern up and could now feel the jitter of his arm muscles that he knew were the first signs of his fear.

"Xavier! Don't mess around." His voice was now shaking out the syllables.

"Come on where are you?" He shouted with a distinct draw of sincere desire to hear his comrades' voice. He heard the sound of a deep breath at the edge of the woods to his right, just before the terrain descended downward. There was a large pile of leaves there just inside the edge of the forest. Oggie approached the pile slowly, and then stopped about 30 to 40 feet away. He held the lantern up higher to cast the reach of the light, then glancing upward into the trees briefly to see there was no visible sky.

Right now Oggie wished he were home, even taking a bath which he despised, but at least he would be safe and might even be having ice cream or heading to his room to read comic books. But no, here he was fulfilling his adventurer spirit, grasping the unknown like his comic book hero's, but at this moment he wished he were with those comic books and forgotten this idea altogether.

Suddenly, he heard the rustle of leaves, and then again. He held the light up higher again, having momentarily let the light drop while he had been thinking of the safety and security of his home. This time the rustling sounds seem to come from beyond the leaf pile, although at this point he couldn't be sure because he couldn't hardly hear anything over the loud thumping and pounding sound emitting from his chest and his head and even from his neck as his heart pulsated with rushes of blood to fuel the driving fear inside him that was swelling up more powerful with each passing moment and seconds. Oggie, knew these sounds, they were the sounds of fear!

"Xavier." He spoke almost normal except for the quiver in his voice. As he approached the pile of leaves, he never even as much as winked for fear of taking his eyes off the pile for even a split second. He stepped slowly closer to the pile, stopping about six feet away. He held the lantern high and squinted his eyes to see what was sticking up from the ground just beyond the leaf pile. He stepped two more steps closer ever so slowly and cautiously tightening his muscles for a springing movement in either direction, left or right or forward or backward should he have to move quickly to get away from whatever fear it was that was rustling leaves and sticks in the forest. He lifted the light higher to see more clearly. It was the bottom of Xavier's tennis shoes. Thank God he thought instantly.

"Xavier, what are you doin' laying down? Let's get the fire goin'."

Xavier did not move. Both feet were pointed up in the air and his body was lying flat on the ground on his back, with arms to his side and face pointed straight up to the treetops. Oggie stood there looking at Xavier then at the leaf pile. Why wasn't Xavier responding? Why didn't it look like he was breathing? He had no answers.

"Xavier, come on!" Demanded Oggie nervously. Xaiver did not move. Oggie moved closer stepping on stones the size of golf balls at the edge of the rim of the incline in the woods, which caused his muscles to quiver and shake as they grasp for a more firm footing.

"You O.K., Xav?" Spoke the quivering voice that moved closer to the leaves. Oggie stretched his head forward of the light to remove the glare of the lantern in his eyes, the lantern now held about head high to improve the lighting of Xavier's lifeless body as it lay there nearly covered by leaves. Oggie's neck stretched as far as it could reach without popping off, to see.

"Xav, what's wrong? His voice echoed with fear. He wished he were home right now. What if something had happened to his buddy? He'd be here all alone! With the body! In the woods! Way back in the cold, dark, woods. ALONE!

The light angled over Xavier's nose and Oggie could now see Xavier's eyes. They were open, looking straight up in the air.

"What are you doing, Xav?" He asked a little more confident now. But there was no answer. Why hadn't Xavier looked toward him when he got within eye range? Why did he not appear to be breathing? These unanswered questions chilled him to the bone, even deep into his spine. He looked intently at Xavier's face. It was expressionless; no life and even looked pale. Was it the light? A rush of chill went through Oggie's body. He was cold now; very cold. He could feel his whole body shivering, yet he just knew that the worse was to come. Alone out here with all these animals and what ever got his buddy.

He quickly swung the light to the left looking behind him then completely turning around he held the light high in the air checking the woods out as far as the lamplight could reach. What was it that caused this? What had gotten Xavier? He stepped one step toward the deeper part of the woods for he thought that he had seen something. It was large and round and close to the ground. A closer step revealed that the object was a large dark rusted brown boulder the size of a 55-gallon drum. He almost breathed a sigh of relief, but a breeze rustled the tree tops making an already eerie condition just a little more chilling. Yes, he just knew he was alone. He began to cry inside. He knew because his eyes were clouding up and he could not see clearly now because of the teary eyed haziness.

Wait a minute; there was a sound to his immediate left. It's where Xavier was. He quickly took that step back and lowered the light. Was Xavier O.K.? Xavier's mouth was slightly open as if the last breath of life had just escaped. Had that been the sound? Oh no! It couldn't be! Xavier's eyes were still open, still fixed straight up into the heavens, into the darkness above them, but Xavier wasn't moving, nor breathing. Oggie was now totally afraid. Fear ran all through him, what had happened to Xavier, and would Oggie find the same demise? As Oggie got down on his knees and sat the lantern on the ground, he purposely leaned his ear toward Xavier and listened for breathing. On his knees he paused to wipe clear the tears that impaired his view even more now. He looked at Xavier's eyes fixed straight ahead.

Did they blink? He thought that they had but he couldn't be sure, because his own eyes were still clouded and blurry. 'Surely they did,' he prayed, 'they just had to have. They just had to!'

Xavier's eyes blinked, then jerked toward Oggie to make eye-to-eye contact. 'He's alive! YES, alive!,' thought Oggie as quickly as if he had been struck by a falling limb. Suddenly, he felt something grab his right leg! Xavier's eyes were focused over Oggie's shoulder, and then Oggie's eyes stretched open wide as Xavier's face screwed up and screamed, at the top of his voice.
"AAHHHHhhhhhhhhhhhhhh!"

CHAPTER 14

WHAT HAPPENED?

Deafened by Xavier's screaming, Oggie spun his head around to look behind him where Xavier had been looking, while fighting to grab at whatever it was that was squeezing his lower leg just above the ankle. His imagination running wild, he swore he could feel teeth, even large sharp teeth. Xavier's screams were intermingled with Oggie's and with both boys screaming, Oggie tried desperately to squint his eyes free of the tears that filled them. It was no use, be it the tears for his friend or the new found ones from fear. All he could see was a blur. Oggie decided in desperation to concentrate on the one single thing that seemed to be creating his greatest fear, and that was whatever it was that was grasping at him the hardest. He grabbed at it and pounded upon it hard, then in the darkness leaned his head forward doubling over and connected his teeth with it and bit with all his might to get free.

"Ooowwl!" Xavier screamed with an intensified scream as the thing which held Oggie released its' grasp.

"Oooouccch!" Oggie jumped free.

"What'd ya' do that for you fool head?" Shouted Xavier holding his arm where Oggie had bitten it.

Oggie shuddered and jumped back a few steps.

"Do what?" He asked.

"You bit me!"

"What? It was you?" Questioned Oggie picking up the lantern from the ground where he had sat it, then knocked it over in all the excitement.

"Sure! Who else could it be?"

"But I thought....."

"Thought what, moron? That some monster was out here lurking in the woods?" Xavier got up and leaned over holding his bitten arm.

"Well, how'd I know?" Replied Oggie in his defense.

Xavier swung around left and right holding on to his arm.

"I think you brought blood."

Oggie stepped toward Xavier a couple steps and held the light up higher to better light Xavier's arm. Sure enough there was blood.

"Look what you've done," Xavier accused, "I'll probably get rabies."

"Hey, I'm sorry Xav," responded Oggie with a concerned voice, "but how did I know it was you."

"Like I said before Og, who else could it have been?"

Oggie thought for a moment then with a screwed up face half yelled back at his friend.

"Wait a minute! You're the one that caused all this. You are the one acting dead or something, then grabbing me and screaming to scare me."

Xavier's mouth fell open with amazement, for seldom did his slower thinking buddy think fast enough to out respond Xavier's wit and aggressiveness.

"And furthermore, this is the second time today! You pee me off Xavier." Oggie spun around swinging the lantern and headed in the direction of the descending grade.

Xavier just knelt there on his knees in awe. 'Could it be that his lesser-witted partner was maturing to become a smarty after all? Would it mean that Xavier would have to sharpen his own wit?'

As Oggie walked on stomping his feet in the decayed forest droppings, he occasionally stopped and shouted back to Xavier to drive his point home.

"Tell ya' what I'm gonna do," he paused long enough to get his thoughts in line, then continued, "First thing tomorrow

I'm gonna pack my stuff and go home." Said he, then turning and continuing his stomping walk.

"I tole' ya' one more time, and that would be it! Well that's it!" He added.

Oggie was upset and he had a right to be. Xavier was continually teasing or playing tricks on him and this one was over the edge. Continuing his stomp to where he thought the campsite was, he held the light lower now to avoid tripping on the fallen branches and undergrowth, especially not wanting to trip carrying a burning kerosene lantern with both fire and fuel in the same container.

"Wait a minute Og," pleaded Xavier getting himself the rest of the way up and rushed a few dashing steps toward the disappearing light, "wait a minute!"

Not listening, Oggie continued at a concentrated pace another 25 or so yards into the blackness with no sign of the campsite clearing ahead.

"Oggie! Stop!" Shouted Xavier demanding his friends' attention as he prepared to run after Oggie.

Oggie stopped and turned toward Xavier's direction. Xavier was standing about 40 feet away by now with his hands on his hips. Oggie raised the lamp to light Xavier's face, if in fact he even could, since there was some distance and as it were his smarter friend was at the edge of the shadowing of the lantern top.

"Exactly where are you going?" Asked Xavier.

Oggie frowned as if to say, 'you know.'

"Back to camp, dumbbell; where else?"

"Well," Xavier paused for a second then continued, "don't you think it would be a good idea to go direct there in this darkness rather than wander around in the forest toward the cliff."

Fortunately for Oggie it was dark and Xavier couldn't see the blush of embarrassment, for though Oggie thought he was headed in the direction of the camp, he was actually heading in the opposite direction, which lead to a cliff with a vertical drop of some 60 to 80 feet. And, at the pace which he was moving, and still a little blurry eyed, Oggie might had ventured off the ledge. Not wanting Xavier to know of his error, Oggie responded with a shaky voice.

"Sure but I wanted to know what was out here before going to sleep."

"Oh, I see," said Xavier, "but would you mind taking me back to camp first."

"Why?" Asked Oggie, "don't you know the way?"

"Sure, it's just that you have the light." Xavier was comforted to reason Oggie's lesser wit.

Oggie breathed a sigh of relief inside, especially now that this moment was over, and commented to himself how dumb he was under his breath, 'Oh, yeah.' He then headed toward Xavier and handed him the lantern.

"You sure you don't mind, Og?"

"What?"

"If we get me back to camp first."

"Oh!" Responded Oggie not wanting Xavier to know that he had absolutely no idea which way to head for camp. Letting loose of the lantern, he tried to sound confident.

"Sure it's O.K., go ahead." Added Oggie as he handed Xavier the lantern.

Xavier turned and headed back toward where they had just been, Oggie following close behind occasionally taking a look behind him, was there something out there following them. Xavier held the light out to his side to both light the trail ahead of him, and also the trail behind him that preceded Oggie. Passing the area of their struggle, Oggie almost asked if this was the place where they had been, but quickly abandoned the idea realizing that he would have revealed his loss of direction to Xavier.

In a few moments the boys surfaced from the woods into the clearing, having stopped along their short distance back to collect some leaves by cupping them against their sides and chest with their hands. At the campsite, they dumped their leaf cargo into the pit, stacked the smaller twigs on top, then lit the leaves with the Blue Top safety matches, which they had packed. As the fire grew, the boys increased the size of twigs they fed the fire, which caused them to seek out larger sized fallen branches and more abundant quantities from the edge of the woods. The fire lit the clearing well enough to see the cliff wall across the pond and the trees at the top of it.

As nightfall progressed, Xavier opened the can of pork & beans and heated dinner in the mess kit pail. Upon reaching the desired temperature, he dumped the contents of the can into their mess kit eating tins, splitting the mess equally between them. Then, after dinner they washed their mess kits in water they collected from the pond and had heated in the mess kit outer pail. During and after dinner they talked about all the great things they had done today, while roasting marshmallows and occasionally breaking into a sort of hysterical laughter over the snake scare when they crossed that part of the day. Then, Xavier reminded them of the woods incident, which resulted in Oggie getting up and heading to the tent.

"Hey, wait a minute, Og," demanded Xavier, "what's up?"

"I'm going to bed!" Said Oggie, disappearing through the tent doors. Then, from inside the tent, Xavier heard Oggie spout back purposefully.

"And tomorrow I'm going home."

Reasoning that he should not press the matter any further, Xavier followed Oggie's lead and both boys closed up the tent and because of both the chill of the cooling night air since the sun sat, and their chilling sun burned arms and faces, they climbed inside their sleeping bags and curled up both wondering if they would fall asleep.

For, as the night fell, a light breeze kicked up, brushing the trees to and fro. The cool air that slipped under the tent against the boys' newfound sunburns caused them to take a chill. And, other than the sound of an occasional mosquito slap and the wind in the trees, the forest was quiet. The forest was now penetrating quiet except for the hoot of a distant owl and an occasional clicking and rattle against the leaves in the woods from a falling twig. Furthermore, not planning to do so but instead talk all night about the next days adventure, the tiredness of the day, the pleasuring swim, and the cool air on their hot faces and arms, the boys quickly slipped off to silent deep sleep, ending an almost perfect day for an explorer. They had hiked away from home, having planned their trip and carried it out in detail. And encountering some adventurous episodes along the way, they had almost lived off the land. Yes, their day had been grand.

CHAPTER 15

NOT SO WELL

While the boys rested quietly all nestled up in their sleeping blankets, having completed their days' journey to their new habitat in the forest, back at home things were not quite so well. By late afternoon that day, Grandpa and Grandma Winfield had conversed with the Bartholomew's as to the whereabouts of their two exploring lads, and from what they could piece together, the boys had gone off for an adventure trip, a trip that had not received the *full* blessing of their parents and guardians respectively, resulting in a scurry through the town as they sought out the two adventurers.

"But how could they?" Asked Grandma Winfield placing her hand over her mouth to cover the frown of her fearful cry. The Bartholomew's and the Winfield's sat in the Winfield country living room with hope and anticipation of a ringing telephone to indicate a resolution to the whereabouts of the boys.

"I didn't think they were really serious," added Mrs. Bartholomew.

"Me either," continued Grandpa Winfield, "I mean, I figured they'd get their camping plans all worked out, but at the last minute I figured they'd give up on the notion or camp in the backyard like before."

Mr. Bartholomew nodded his head in agreement, "that's what I figured, too and when Gloria (Mrs. Bartholomew) mentioned it at the dinner table and I even talked with Oggie about how much fun I'd had on some of my camping experiences, I just shelved the idea not thinking he was really serious about it. Really, I kind of ignored the whole thing. I just didn't think they were really serious."

"Oh my Lord!" They're all alone out there some where!" Burst Mrs. Bartholomew in tears, cupping her face in her hands and swaying forward and backward.

"My little baby is all alone in the woods." She began to cry as Mr. Bartholomew moved closer to his wife.

"Oh my Lord," added Grandma Winfield, she too dropping her head into her cupped hands giving way to the drawing urge for tears.

Mr. Bartholomew leaned over to his wife wrapping his left arm around her shoulders, drawing her near.

"They'll be fine baby. They're together."

"Why sure," added Grandpa Winfield sitting on the arm of Grandma Winfield's chair.

"If there's anyone who could fend for themselves, it's definitely that Xavier and Oggie. Why, I'd take them boys over any man in this town if it came to push or shove. They'll be fine."

"You sure Mr. Winfield?" Asked Mrs. Bartholomew, through sniffs wanting desperately to feel even a slice of hope.

"You sure Paps?" Inquired Grandma Winfield, using the title she gave him when grasping for security.

Trying to reassure the female gender, Grandpa Winfield told a couple stories about Xavier and Oggie, revealing their ingenious wit. Yet, deep down inside he too worried about the boys. After all, it was that time of the year when rabies ran rampant with skunks, foxes, and wolves. Then of course there was the vicious activity of the local black bear, especially this time of year when the black bear tried to consume all the calories they could in order to put on a nice layer of fat for winter.

"Think we should call Bobby, Mr. Winfield?" Asked Mr. Bartholomew referring to their local constabulary.

"Naw, I don't think we need to," responded he, winking in agreement without the women knowing.

"You're probably right." Reaffirmed Mr. Bartholomew, motioning his head to the kitchen.

After a few words of comforting exchange with the women, Grandpa Winfield offered Mr. Bartholomew a coffee in the kitchen drawing the men from the living room to the large country kitchen of the older Winfield house.

"What shall we tell Bobby?" Asked Mr. Bartholomew.

"Well, I really do think that the boys will be fine. Maybe a little scared tonight if they don't come in, but we ought to let Bobby know so maybe he could be on the look out for our little comrades walking home in the middle of the night." Mr. Winfield tried to at least provide a comforting thought.

"I'm a little concerned for, Oggie. I don't think he's ever been out like this."

"Well now," continued the experienced elder, "those boys have slept overnight with each other many times; even in that ole shed out back."

Not wanting to reveal his real concerns, Mr. Winfield added, "They'll be fine Thomas."

"You're probably right. You wanna call Bobby?"

"Sure. But I think maybe it'd be better if I went over to his house. You know, the phone conversation being overhead by the worried ears in the other room."

"Sure," said Mr. Bartholomew lifting his coffee cup to his lips and tilting his head forward for a warming sip, "I'll keep peace here. Why not go ahead, I'd feel a lot better."

Grandpa Winfield set down his cup and turned to lift his keys to the old '56 Buick that was parked in the three-sided garage out back next to the utility shed where Xavier and Oggie had discovered all their camping imaginations.

"Tell the women folk that I'm taking a stroll through town to look for the boys. But, avoid mentioning night fall or the police."

"Will do," nodded Mr. Bartholomew as Winfield slipped out the door quietly. "Harold's going to take a run through town," spouted Mr. Bartholomew returning to the room. He spoke with confidence for the benefit of his wife and Grandma Winfield. He sat by his wife and wrapped his arm around her.

"Mrs. Bartholomew and I will stay here until Harold returns," Mr. Bartholomew assured Grandma Winfield, as the three of them heard the old Buick drive out the lane.

"Great," offered back Mrs. Winfield.

CHAPTER 16

MORE TROUBLE

As Grandpa Winfield maneuvered the old Buick through town, he looked along the sidewalks and alleys in hopes of catching a glimpse of the boys returning home. He thought about the conversation he and Xavier had had the day before and how he wished he had the confidence of safety that he had felt then. He was most fearful of his worst thoughts of what could actually happen to the boys.

Along the way to the house of the Chief of Police, he passed two different State Police vehicles, arousing his suspicions of their frequency in the small and sparsely populated community of Chestnut Ridge. 'Perhaps,' he reasoned, 'it was just coincidence or his often curious nature' the latter of which was a trait that Xavier also shared. As he tried to flee these thoughts, he rounded a big curve to the right entering the East End section of town. Then, to the first street on the left, then up the slight incline, bearing left at the top of the incline straight ahead to the little house immediately on the left at the corner of Beacon and Maple. This small one story cottage was the residence of Mr. Robert Malcum, their Chief and only Policeman of the village.

Mrs. Malcum came to the door with a cup of coffee offering Grandpa Winfield the same as she invited him in.

"Are you sure Harold? I just made it." The shoulder length brown haired and brown eyed Mrs. Malcum asked.

"Thank you but I'm just fine."

Mrs. Malcum explained that Chief Malcum was doing his rounds through town and would be back around 9:00 pm.

Looking at his watch, Grandpa Winfield calculated about 30 minutes.

"Maybe I will take that coffee after all if you don't mind my waiting?"

"No problem. Is it urgent that you speak with my husband, Mr. Winfield?" Asked Mrs. Malcum, turning into their small living room and motioning for Grandpa Winfield to take a seat.

"Well," paused Grandpa Winfield, looking down to sure his footing while heading to the couch along the outside wall in front of the two front windows.

"I really don't think it's anything, but my grandson and his buddy haven't come home from a trip that they left for early this mornin'."

"I guess that's urgent enough," said Mrs. Malcum stopping her motion to sit in an easy chair across from Grandpa Winfield and then returning upright.

"You wait here and I'll be right back, O.K.?"

"Yes ma'am," replied her senior.

"No problem," said she turning toward the kitchen. After clearing the foyer, she stopped and turned toward her guest and opened her mouth to take a breath to ask a question. But, before she could ask.

"Regular," spoke Mr. Winfield, which is to mean with cream and sugar.

"Just what I was going to ask," she replied and with that she slipped into the kitchen.

While sitting in the living room alone, Grandpa Winfield rested his face in his hands and pondered about where his dear little Xavier could be. He presumed that they'd planned to go to the old Winfield farm, but reasoned that the boys couldn't take all the gear which he had seen them collect over the past couple days. These thoughts caused him to wonder why he hadn't checked the shed to see if in fact the gear was gone. Maybe the boys never really went at all and were just out late. 'Not likely,' he reasoned shaking his head in hand, 'Xavier was full of unusual activity for a boy his age, but being out late was not one of them.' Grandpa reasoned that Xavier was a boy of his word and if he had said they were going camping, then for sure that's where they were. Why hadn't he listened closer to Xavier? 'Perhaps the big ole hill behind the house,' he thought, 'Xavier loved hiking up that hill and taking in the mammoth view of Chestnut Ridge as the town could be viewed from the south ridge. Yes,' he continued, 'that must be where they are.' His thoughts were interrupted by the sound of a faint voice from the other side of the wall, in the kitchen. It was Chief Malcum's wife. 'Who on earth could she be talking too?' He thought. The Chief and she had no children. 'Did she have a guest? And, had he interrupted their visit?' No sooner had he decided to investigate than Mrs. Malcum returned to the room cupping an ivory white ceramic cup with both her hands. She headed direct to Grandpa Winfield.

"One cup of fresh coffee with cream and sugar sir," said Mrs. Malcum extending her hands toward the rising elder Winfield. "Just brewed it about fifteen minutes ago. Chief likes a fresh cup when he returns from his early rounds."

"Early rounds?" Questioned Grandpa Winfield. "Why I'm usually headed to bed shortly after this hour."

"Well, Bobby has to go out again for the late round at 10:30 or 11:00."

"Oh, sure. Sorry I forgot."

"It's O.K. Most people forget that in a small one officer town, the police Chief has to do all the policing."

"I'm sorry." Apologized Grandpa Winfield, "most of us just don't even think how it all gets done."

"It's O.K. You needn't apologize. If he weren't my husband, I wouldn't know either," said she chuckling a little, taking a seat and picking up her own cup of coffee and taking a slow sip.

"Thank you for the coffee."

"You're very welcome," she replied.

Grandpa Winfield smiled thinking how fortunate their town was to have such servants as the Malcum's who had come to their quaint little village settling for much less money than the other offers that had been *tendered* this ten year military veteran of the Second World War.

"While I was in the kitchen, I radioed Bobby and he'll be right here," said Mrs. Malcum, interrupting Grandpa Winfield's thoughts.

"What?" He asked, trying to digest what she had said.

"I called Bobby on our city radio in the other room and he'll be here in about two or three minutes. He was just passing by the Elementary school on Randolph."

"You have a radio here?"

"Sure, it's the one that used to be at the city building. But with the radio there the only one that could use it was the City Secretary during the day. But since most of the need for the Chief is in the evening or night, the town Board approved moving it here so I could call him on it."

"Well, that's great," said the old man, relieved to know that help was on the way.

"Doesn't it bother you though? I mean.......having to interrupt your evening or night to take care of other peoples problems?"

"No, not really. A job like this is a way of life for a one-policeman town. Besides, they also rigged the phone at the City building so that when they're not there, they switch it to a new phone in our kitchen. That way, calls for Bobby come directly here and if he's out, I can now get any new call right to him without delay."

Amazed at the service of the Malcum's, Mr. Winfield had to comment.

"Thank you Mrs. Malcum for calling Bobby, and especially for you and your husband yielding your lives to Chestnut Ridge so gracious as you have."

"Why thank you Mr. Winfield."

No sooner had the words left her lips, than did they heard the sound of a car rustling the gravels in the driveway next to the house, which Grandpa Winfield had been careful not to block. Grandpa Winfield nearly spilled his coffee turning to look out the front windows. Sure enough, it was Chief Malcum in the town's only police cruiser, sporting the traditional red rotating beacon light on the roof of an all black car with a golden badge medallion print on both driver and passenger car doors boasting the towns police symbol. Grandpa Winfield quickly turned back around and took a long slow sip of his coffee to moisten his mouth.

"Coffee's good Mrs. Malcum."

"Why thank you sir," replied Mrs. Malcum, "just stay seated and I'll get Chief a cup and the two of you can sit and talk out the situation."

"Thank you ma'am."

"You're welcome, sir."

Chief Malcum entered the room through the front door ducking to avoid contact with the top of the doorframe. He was a tall man of 6'3" having curly short black hair and dark Italian looking complexion. His face was long and slender. Holding his uniformed flat-rimmed hat at his side, Chief Malcum stepped into the living room from the foyer. Grandpa Winfield maneuvered his elderly frame as if to get up, to which Chief Malcum held his hand out toward Winfield.

"Please stay seated Mr. Winfield. I'll have a seat right here beside you and you can tell me everything." Chief Malcum stepped his long slender frame to the armchair beside the couch to the left of Grandpa Winfield. Grandpa admired the smell of the leather of the gun belt and the uniform that Chief Malcum was almost always to be seen in.

"Well Bobby, I don't know if it's anythin' or not, but you see my grandson and his buddy been plannin' this camping trip see?" Grandpa Winfield paused for confirmation from the Chief.

"That would be Xaiver and the Bartholomew boy right?"

"Yes sir, Oggie."

"O.K., go on." Chief Malcum nodded his head.

"Well, they talked about going on this camping trip somewhere but we didn't actually think they'd really do it, you know?" Continued Harold Winfield.

"Sure," replied Chief Malcum, "but then that Xavier's quite an enterprising young man as I recall."

"Yes sir, he sure is."

The Chief continued, "Yeah, he's a boy you can trust. If he says he's up to something, you can bet he'll do it."

"Yes sir that's him." Added Grandpa Winfield taking another sip of coffee.

"Well sir, they left this mornin' see?" Mrs. Malcum entered the room with a matching cup to the one that Grandpa Winfield and she had. Grandpa Winfield started to get up as she entered the room, but she insisted that he remain seated, and then she handed the cup to her husband, who in turn winked at her and nodded his head to thank her for the coffee.

"Thanks honey," said he smiling at her.

"Would you like me to stay in the other room, hon?" Mrs. Malcum asked her husband.

"Mr. Winfield?" Asked Chief Malcum directing the question to him.

"Naw. Shucks, you might even be able to help." Mrs. Malcum took the seat across from Grandpa Winfield that she had secured earlier, picked up her own cup and took another sip.

"Do go on Mr. Winfield," said Chief Malcum glancing at his wristwatch.

"Well anyway, here tis' about 8:30 or 9:00 and the boys aren't back."

"Yes sir, it's about 8:50. The sun was just setting securely as I came in. Bet them boys are roasting hot dogs or marshmallows about now," said the Chief lifting his cup to sip in a soft warm draw.

"Do ya' think we're fretting over nothing?"

"No sir. Got to be cautious you know?" Continued Chief Malcum, Grandpa nodding an acceptance to what he had just asked.

"Can you tell me what you think the boys have with them, and what they're wearing when you last saw them?" Continued the Chief.

Grandpa thought carefully and proceeded to give Chief Malcum as accurate a description as he could remember as well as the items that he was almost certain that they had taken.

"I mean, I haven't even checked to see that the camping gear is gone out of the shed. Maybe it's still there and they haven't even gone."

"Oh you can check Mr. Winfield, but my guess is that those boys are exploring your dads' old farm. Xavier and you used to go up there all the time didn't you?"

"Yes sir, we sure did, till I took that tumble August past."

"Why I remember that, had to take you to the hospital myself remember?"

"Yes sir, I sure do. Like to thank you again for that Bobby."

They both chuckled being reminded how last August Grandpa Winfield fell down the second floor stairs hardly taking an injury at all. However, his left knee acted up a little since. All three took a sip of Mrs. Malcum's excellent coffee in unison.

"I'll bet your wife is worried sick," asked Chief Malcum.

"Yes sir, I tried to comfort her, but I don't know that I quite know what to do under the circumstances. You know that boy means the world to us."

"How about the Bartholomew's? Have you talked to them?"

"Yes sir, they are with my wife right now."

"Well, why don't we finish our coffee then take some passes through town, then go to your house and talk to Mrs. Winfield to help settle her concerns."

"Sure," responded Grandpa Winfield with an almost peaceful breath.

"You can leave your car out front and I'll come get you in the mornin'"

"Well, that'd be great if it's no bother. Don't see so well after dark anymore you know?"

"Yes sir," chuckled Chief Malcum, "no problem and I do know what you mean about seeing after dark. We all get there some day, huh?"

They chuckled, drank their coffee, and left after Chief Malcum gave his wife a hug and kiss.

Having not seen any whereabouts of the boys during their scanning drive through town, they proceeded to the Winfield's. At the Winfield's Chief Malcum comforted Grandma Winfield and Mrs. Bartholomew by assuring them that everything would be just fine. Moreover, he explained that there was a storm coming through tonight, but that they need not to worry because he was sure that the boys were set up so that they'd be well protected reassuring them where he could. They accepted these words of comfort somewhat reluctantly, but at the closing of their conversations, promised the Chief that they'd rest knowing that his faith and trust in the boys safety equaled what they too believed of the boys. Chief Malcum resounded that assurance explaining that he had had several opportunities to chat with Xavier and Oggie on occasions when he would encounter the boys about Chestnut Ridge wrapped up and involved in one of their enterprising ideas, when they had not even realized they had an observer. Chief Malcum assured the Winfield's and Bartholomew's that the boys were safe; while also, sharing with them a couple of the most enterprising stories of the boys' wit that he had experienced to gain their confidence in the boys' ingenuity and safety.

CHAPTER 17

GOOD NEWS AND BAD NEWS

Upon leaving the Winfield house, Chief Malcum scouted about town in search of the missing boys ending his round at the old Winfield farm lane. Using his flashlight to light the way in the dark, Chief Malcum walked the incline lane looking for signs of the boys' passage. To his satisfaction, sure enough there in the sandy *loam* of the old mining lane were tennis shoe footprints and tire prints of a wagon. He proceeded up the lane toward where the old house used to be and continually was catching glimpses of the boys trail at every spot where eroded soil had allowed a dust print in the soft powdery sandy like spoiled topsoil. Had he waited until tomorrow, the forecasted rain that was sure to come tonight would surely have removed this valuable evidence of the boy's whereabouts. The Chief assured himself of his expectations of the boy's whereabouts. As he moved up the lane, a wind was beginning to kick up in the trees. It was one of those winds in which one knew that rain was not far away. He stopped and flashed the light up in the big old oak, which had been shade to Xavier and Oggie earlier that day, and observed the leaves turning over revealing their underside. The Chief reasoned that a storm would definitely pass their way tonight, for even the trees' leaves were turning over providing a sure sign that they were preparing for a drink.

Chief Malcum stepped upon the concrete portion of the old front porch where the farmhouse had been, stepping carefully as not to fall through the weather rotted floor planks on the wooden portion of the remaining porch. The cellar had been filled with soil, which pleased the Chief since he had asked the Winfield's a couple times to fill the hole that represented a safety risk if someone were to go wandering there at night. Moreover, he hadn't wanted to burden the aged Winfield's but was pleased that the risk was gone.

Carefully stepping back off the porch, Chief Malcum proceeded to the part of the lane that headed directly to the woods. Nearly losing his footing a couple times in the rutted lane he stepped to the opposite side of the lane, which had been the side revealing the tracks earlier. Stepping carefully, Malcum proceeded cautiously watching where he stepped so as not to step on any tracks, were he to find any, until he came to an area in which the grass was nearly exhausted completely. Sure enough, there were two separate types of footprints in the sandy clay soil, plus tire tracks of what was surely the wagon that Mr. Winfield had mentioned. He concluded that this must be the same wagon that he had seen Xavier and Oggie pulling a couple days earlier filled with empty pop bottles. 'Yes,' he reasoned, 'the boys whereabouts were truly known.' He assured himself that an early morning search would be much more fruitful and proceeded back to the police cruiser, detailing in his mind a search plan.

Arriving home, Chief Malcum informed his wife concerning the Winfield matter following which he learned that the State Police had phoned to place him on alert that there was a manhunt for two escaped prisoners from the State Correction facility near Chicolton, OH. An abandoned car depleted of fuel had been discovered about five miles north of Chestnut Ridge that matched the identity of one reported stolen only hours after the escape in Chicolton, and although there was no physical evidence supporting the suspicion of the State Police theory that this abandon car was in fact driven there by the escaped criminals, the possibilities were quite convincing.

"This is not good," the Chief told his wife.

"I know," she said then added, "Should you tell the Winfield's?"

"First things first. Learn of the current status regarding the escapees, then proceed accordingly." With that the Chief proceeded to the phone to call the State Police.

The Chief called the Ohio State Police Post in Jamestown, just twelve miles to the north of Chestnut Ridge on State Route 95, to confirm the details and present status of the escapees while informing them of the missing children. Together Chief Malcum and Sergeant George Scott of the State Police barracks pieced together a search plan for the next morning and with the day nearing its' end, the Chief and his wife headed for bed.

Meanwhile however, back in the woods the unsuspecting boys were sound asleep as the night creatures carried on about their nightly instinctive activities. A deer passed within six or eight feet of their tent stopping for a moment to investigate the unfamiliar snoring sounds emerging from the boys' tent. Inside the tent, Oggie snorted which startled the deer causing it to snort and hightail it for less active surroundings, the launching action nearly waking Oggie.

However, less concerned for the snoring inside the tent was a family of raccoons who were treating themselves to Twinkie cakes, chocolate cookies, marshmallows, and any bread that could easily be retrieved from the boys camping gear. In addition, to these uninvited guests, there was a visit from a much larger creature of the night species. When this one occasioned the boys camp, the raccoons departed straightaway, letting this creature finish off the remains which were inaccessible by the smaller paws of the coon. Yes, to this master, the camping gear was no match or challenge to his powerful paws and arms allowing him to easily open any canvas or package in order to feed on this new food source.

Without a doubt the night belongs to the animals, and thus while Xavier and Oggie slept, the night creatures explored the newness of the boys' *paraphernalia*, taking or sampling as they desired, the boys hearing none of it because of the night chill, their tiredness, and the almost silent serenity that filled their minds and souls.

As predicted by Chief Malcum, a severe thunderstorm swept through Chestnut Ridge during the night. However, fortunate for our Xavier and Oggie, only the northern edge of the storm passed overhead their area resulting in merely medium rainfall although a significant amount of wind; and fortunate for the boys, not strong enough to crack loose the large dead limb in the Chestnut tree behind their tent, for had it broken off, the size and weight of it would surely have injured one or both of the boys.

For nearby Chestnut Ridge though the storm poured mountains of rainfall with fierce lightning and thunder. Had the two lads been awake, the light show would have been stupendous. But for the two tired heavy sleepers alone in the sheltered woods, a quiet cozy rainfall made the sleeping even the more accommodating.

Back in Chestnut Ridge, the Winfield's and Bartholomew's slept poorly their minds constantly reminding them of how afraid the boys must be, especially in light of the thunderstorm. Mrs. Bartholomew woke imagining how the boys must be hugging the most unsafe thing in the woods during a lightning storm, a tree. As the wind blew furiously against their house and the lightning cracked, Mrs. Winfield shuttered to think of her precious grandson alone and afraid in that great big, dark, cold forest, and how infinitely small the boys where in comparison to the massive forest and the power of the thunderstorm. Each family member in their own way, prayed a prayer, each including a request to God that He would protect their innocent children and grandchildren respectively and reminded themselves each in their own way by question, 'if only they had listened to the boys!'

Xavier woke for just a moment when a period of larger raindrops struck the tent roof and penetrated through the dried out, uncoated, canvas and peppered his face with a spray of sprinkles. 'How fitting,' he thought, 'the perfect backdrop for a most restful sleep.' Rolling over, Xavier slumbered back off into the deep darkness of sleep, while outside the most feared creature of the woods finished off the last of the boys' accessible perishable goods, pausing for only a moment when Xavier turned over inside the tent, which caught the creatures attention. The creature started to investigate the large canvas structure that housed the two sleeping lads, however the unfamiliar sounds emitting from the tent were strange enough that the creature chose to avoid investigating. Moreover, since the boys were snuggled deep inside their sleeping bags the smell of blood that this creature sought was covered from his nostrils.

CHAPTER 18

THE SEARCH BEGINS

SLAP!! The silence was broken. Xavier's eyes jerked open wide. It was hot inside the tent. Xavier looked toward where the sound had come from and observed Oggie waving his arms about in the air over him at a single fly that was intent on pestering him eternally.

"Wow, is it warm or what?" Asked Xavier.

"Yeah, sure is. Feels good," replied Oggie.

"Boy I..aaahhh slept," said Xavier with a widening mouth to let out a nice morning yawn.

"Yea, except I got cold last night."

"What?"

"I got cold last night. Like real cold."

Xavier lifted up on one arm toward his plump friend.

"Well you sure couldn't tell it. I woke during the rain and you were snoring."

"I was not," popped Oggie in defense stoutly.

"Yea you were? In fact, you probably woke me."

"Rain?" Asked Oggie.

"Yea, it rained last night."

Oggie got up and untied the tent door flaps and attempted to poke his head outside. When the chill of the cooler morning air hit him in the face he ducked back in, closing the flaps behind him, and snuggled back inside the sleeping bag.

"It's cold outside!"

"Baloney," said Xavier climbing out of his own sleeping bag to check, wherein like Oggie earlier, without even getting the flap completely open to look outside, he quickly crawled back on all fours to his own bag and snuggled back inside where it was warm. Moreover, they tried to stay awake, but it being so peaceful, and warm in their respective bags, and still tired from yesterday's extenuating efforts, the boys dozed off for another hour or so.

Xavier and Oggie were both awakened early by the distant sound of Chief Malcum's voice hollering for the two boys. Malcum had been on the hunt for the boys since early that morning; early twilight to be exact. However, the erasing rain had seriously affected his search. No tracks were to be found anywhere; still, Chief Malcum followed the old mining trail calling out the boys' names occasionally, which they had unknowingly heard. Malcum had arrived at the older Winfield farm at 7:30 am for a little pre-investigative effort, hoping of course that he might find the boys and take them to their families, the latter of whom were anxious to see the likes of them. He had walked the distance to the large open mining area which was the last area excavated. And even thought there was a strong quick drying north wind, insufficient drying time was causing him to step carefully to avoid muddy erosion pools which lay quietly awaiting to be disturbed by an intruder in the calm of the early morning forest. These were the same type of pools that yesterday evening revealed the trail of the boys, but were now filled with water. Moreover, now washed away, the crossover point where the boys had taken the turn into the grown over entrance to the earliest of the strip mine areas, the rain washed roadbed left no clue as to where the boys had trailed. Thus, it was anyone's guess as to where the boys had trailed off to.

Unable to find any signs of the boys, Chief Malcum drove to the Winfield's house and continued his verbal inquiry of the woods.

"Mr. Winfield?" Inquired Chief Malcum loudly through the screen at the back door of the old Winfield home.

"I coming," hollered a weak voice from inside the house.

"It's Malcum," replied Chief Malcum assuming that the frail voice would be none other than the elder Mrs. Winfield. She appeared in the kitchen from the doorway that lead to the living room.

"Oh have you found them?" Pleaded Mrs. Winfield.

"No ma'am but I need to talk to your husband."

"What is it?" She asked her voice trailing softer into a pale plea.

"Nothing ma'am, I just need some help with the woods."

"Any signs of the boys?"

"Nothing yet ma'am, but the rain has washed away any signs of their trail, so I need Mr. Winfield to help me navigate the trails."

"Oh yes, the rain, I bet the boys were scared to death" said she nodding her head back and forth.

"Mr. Winfield Ma'am?"

"Oh yes, of course," said she opening the door to let the Chief in.

"I'm sorry, look at me just standing here asking questions. He's on the telephone, I'll just give him a holler." She hollered the elder Winfield's name and continued her discussion with Chief Malcum, giving another holler after a lapse of less than a minute, wherein Mr. Winfield appeared presto.

"What is it?" Inquired he rounding the corner of the entry from the living room.

"Oh, Chief Malcum. Tell me you have some good news my man."

"Well sir, what I have is need of your services to assist the navigation."

"Sure, that mining company sure made a mess of things huh?"

"Yes sir, and the rain sure didn't help."

"Sure, the footprints are gone huh?"

"Yes sir."

Mr. Winfield turned to his worried foot-and-a-half-shorter wife then gave her a kiss on the forehead.

"We'll be back Puggs." (A nickname that Grandpa Winfield offen called Grandma Winfield.

"Find those boys Harold!" Said she with a quiver in her voice.

"I'll be back to check on you in a while Puggs." And with that, the two men left in Chief Malcum's police car.

"I believe I'm on the wrong side of the woods Mr. Winfield." Said Chief Malcum turning his head toward Mr. Winfield. But Mr. Winfield looked straight ahead without answer signifying that he was deep in some form of thought. After a pause of silence he answered.

"Huh.... What?"

"No need to worry Mr. Winfield. The boys are fine."

"No I was just trying to remember if the dynamite was ever removed from the old storage shed."

"What Dynamite?"

"There was this old cement block building at the split of the road which used to hold dynamite for blasting. But I think that it was emptied many years back. It seems so long ago."

"Why worry about the dynamite now, Mr. Winfield?"

Grandpa Winfield turned his head toward Chief Malcum as the Chief turned his and the two men's eyes connected.

"Xavier," said they in unison as their heads offered confirming nods. Not realizing so, Chief Malcum touched the throttle pedal to the engine just a little harder.

Arriving at the old Winfield farm, Chief Malcum pulled the police cruiser up to the edge of the woods and started to turn the engine off, having just finished radioing his wife to give her an update. But, just before switching the key off, the radio sounded.

"Chief Malcum; over." He and Winfield looked at each other in amazement.

"Chief Malcum. This is the State Police; over." Malcum picked up the microphone and turned up the volume on the radio.

"10-4 this is Malcum; over."

"10-4 Malcum. This is Sergeant George Scott of Unit 38 I spoke with you last night; over."

Pressing the microphone button cautiously as he held up a finger to silence the sharpening astute of Grandpa Winfield.

"10-4 Sergeant Scott, I have subject Winfield with me and we're at the *rendezvous* meet; 10-4?"

Grandpa Winfield interrupted, "the state police?"

Malcum held up a couple fingers toward the elder gentleman to silence him for just a moment while they listened.

"10-4 Malcum. We'll have two units join you momentarily; over and out." The squelch of the radio echoed.

"There's more than one unit?" Asked Winfield. But before the Chief could respond, Winfield added nervously, "the boys aren't really lost Bobby, we just think they ought to be at home. We don't need State Police." It was as much a statement as a posed question to Bobby that they didn't need to make a state matter of the missing boys.

"Yes sir I know and I don't want to alarm you, but we have a situation here at the moment."

"What?" Grandpa's ears moved up and back in alarm as his eyebrows rose slightly.

Chief Malcum gathered his thoughts carefully.

"I didn't want to bring this up at your home in front of Mrs. Winfield, but a car was discovered this morning about five miles north of here which is believed to have been stolen by two escaped criminals from Southern State Correction facility and are believed to be somewhere near here or just north of here."

Grandpa gasped a couple of short breaths.

"Whaa?....." The elder Winfield asked.

"Please Mr. Winfield, don't get alarmed. We need you to focus and help find the boys. And, besides, there's no reason to believe that these men are even dangerous so far as we know. They were serving time for some petty crime."

"Petty crime and state convicts. What on earth was I thinking? I am partly responsible for these boys getting excited about this camping idea. Oh my...."

Recognizing Mr. Winfield's guilt, Chief Malcum interrupted and offered some assurance.

"Well Mr. Winfield, who could have known that this would be the weekend of an escape? And, who's to say that the criminals are even in this county for that matter."

"Yea, you're right Bobby. Let's go find those boys and get em' home safe," nodded Mr. Winfield.

In the lapse of about fifteen minutes, two State Police cruisers rolled up the drive revealing four state police officers. Chief Malcum and Grandpa Winfield had exited the police cruiser and walked toward the other police units, as the officers exited their respective vehicles, one walking straight toward Malcum and Winfield, the other three proceeding to the trunk of the forward most vehicle.

"Good morning. Chief Malcum I presume?" Said a tall dark complexioned man reaching his right hand toward Chief Malcum.

"Sergeant Scott of District 14 Post 3." The two men shook hands.

"Pleasure to meet you sir," greeted Malcum, as he turned toward Grandpa Winfield, "this is Mr. Harold Winfield who we spoke about on the telephone last night."

Grandpa Winfield offered his right hand and the two shook hands.

"Pleasure to meet you Sergeant."

"Pleasure to meet you sir," said Sergeant Scott turning to the three other officers as they joined Malcum, Winfield, and Scott. The three officers were carrying short-muzzled pump shotguns. Sergeant Scott proceeded to introduce Malcum and Winfield, to each other and each nodding his head toward them consecutively as each man offered his hand for a handshake also. They were: Trooper John Hart, Trooper Alex Cheerman, and Trooper Ben Davis. Upon Grandpa Winfield offering each his pleasure of their meeting, Sergeant introduced each of his associates to Chief Malcum.

"Please don't be alarmed. The weapons are precautionary." Offered Sergeant Scott.

"Understood." Nodded Malcum

"Suggestions?" Inquired Sergeant Scott humbly.

"Well sir," said Malcum, "I thought Mr. Winfield could give us some clue as to navigating these woods and we could plan a search and rescue from there."

"Sounds good," nodded Sergeant Scott lifting a large folded paper in his left hand pointing it toward the rear trunk of Chief Malcum's police cruiser. As all the men walked toward the cruiser Scott unfold what appeared to be a large map. The map was a topographical map that displayed roads, houses, and elevations of the land. It looked much like a weather map with swirls of lines and curves representing altitudes of hills and valleys. Spreading out the map, the Sergeant pointed to a spot on the map.

"I believe we are about here." Pointed Sergeant Scott.

Chief Malcum studied the map for a moment placing several landmarks in his mind.

"That appears to be about right sir." Malcum affirmed.

Again pointing at the map where a red X was marked, Sergeant offered, "this is the approximate location of the discovered stolen car."

Chief Malcum searched the highway markings penciled on the map carefully.

"I thought the car was found on Saw Mill Road?" Queried he.

"That's correct sir. Why?"

"Well, I believe that that X is marked on Canada Hill Road. This is Saw Hill Road," said Malcum pointing to a road closer to where they were at the moment.

"Are you sure?" Asked Sergeant Scott looking directly at Chief Malcum, then at each of the respective other officers.

"Well, this is the water tower," said Malcum pointing to a circle on the map, "and this is the first intersection south of that water tower." He motioned to a spot on the map.

"That is Canada Hill Road, named after the group that left our town in the late 1800's to go to Canada to seek their venture in gold and oil." Pointed out the Chief.

"O.K. I remember that road it's at a curve at the foot of the hill where the tower is, right?" The Sergeant again looked up from the map at Chief Malcum.

"That's right sir, it's at a curve." Malcum confirmed.

"The car was *not* found on that road, but was the next one south; isn't that correct Trooper Davis?" Asked he leaning forward to look around Troopers Hart and Cheerman to look directly at Trooper Davis.

"That's correct sir. It was the second road on the right from the bottom of the hill. And, it wasn't a four way intersection as is indicated on the map; it was a three way with a turn offered only to the right as you would go south."

"Well then, I've placed the X in the wrong location." Pointed out Scott. After making this statement and nodding his head toward Trooper Cheerman, Cheerman turned and headed toward the cruiser that he and Sergeant Scott had come from, while the remaining men discussed the terrain, Trooper Cheerman retrieved a red marking pencil from the cruiser and placed a radio message on their state frequency, before returning to the group and giving the red pencil to Sergeant Scott.

Trooper Cheerman placed a red X on the map where Sergeant Scott had pointed moments ago, the same location that Chief Malcum had indicated as the correct road, this being the location of where the stolen car had been found, marking out the original incorrect location.

"Well now, it appears that the car is closer to where we are now, and it is well to believe then that our subjects are in these woods ahead of us." Said the Sergeant looking up from the map toward the woods that lay ahead of them.

Grandpa exhausted his lungs in a gasp and shook his head back and forth with a frown.

"It's OK Mr. Winfield," comforted Chief Malcum, "we're on the boys trail now and with you by our side sir we're sure to find them pronto." The elder gentleman just shook his head back and forth.

"Their in the Good Lord's hands, Chief Malcum," said Winfield looking at the Chief and changing his nod to an affirming one.

"I trust that He will look over them." The other men looked at each other with agreeing expressions.

"I have units patrolling the areas north, south, and west of us...." Began Sergeant Scott.

Trooper Davis interrupted briefly, "Sorry to interrupt sir, but I radioed the road correction sir."

"Very well. Thanks Davis. As I was saying," continued Scott this time pointing to the map in a circular squared off motion, "we have units patrolling these roads heavily, six in all plus two State Corrections units. So, we've pretty much isolated the area to the large hilly woods before us. So, what can you tell us about these woods Mr. Winfield."

"Harold if you will," offered Mr. Winfield politely, not knowing that it was required procedure of a state police official to use sir and ma'am when addressing the respective genders.

"Yes sir," responded the Sergeant retrieving the red pencil from Cheerman and handing it to Winfield.

Grandpa Winfield proceeded to point on the map and carefully mark upon it the excavation mining roads and landmarks like the dynamite house as best as he could remember. He then adjusted his bifocals and pressing lighter marked a square at a curve to the left and then a road off to the left near the end of the main road.

"Yes, I walked that far," offered Chief Malcum. "What is in here?" He pointed to the void area to the left of the main roadbed and to the left of the left branch road.

"That's the second stripping area," said Winfield pointing to the intersection again, then continuing, "this area was second to strip then the longer older road."

He then pointed at the straight section of the long main road, "This was much later; maybe eight years or so later. So, most of it grew up in here." He pointed to the area to the left of the branch road.

"However, most of this is fairly new," he pointed at the end of the main road.

"But the first part is the most treacherous," he pointed to the area off to the right of the main road and to the right of the square which he had drawn.

"The old dynamite shed right?" Asked Chief Malcum pointing at the square that Winfield had sketched upon the paper.

"Yes sir. Just before here," he pointed at the shed and where the curve to the left was, "is where the oldest road is, the old stripping area. Those are much smaller strip benches, but several of them, have ponds." He then marked with a pencil a road off to the right of the main road well before the shed and just before the curve to the left.

The Chief looked at the area carefully and pointed to the newly marked road Winfield had drawn.

"I didn't see that road." Said he.

"No Bobby, that roads almost grown up."

"I suggest we begin here," said the chief pointing to the area of that last road marked upon the map by Mr. Winfield.

"How about you and I, search that area, while Troopers Hart and Davis search the area off to the left," instructed Sergeant Scott, "while Trooper Cheerman and Mr. Winfield await further units."

"Sounds like a good plan to me," offered Chief Malcum, though he knew that the Sergeant was only offering Malcum's approval out of courtesy for this was a state police matter which meant that the local constabulary had no authority or jurisdiction in the matter.

"Would you like me to come along?" Asked Grandpa Winfield.

"No sir," inserted Sergeant Scott, just as Chief Malcum was preparing to answer.

"We need you here sir in the event that someone needs us. Trooper Davis get us the portables."

Trooper Davis charted off to retrieve the portable radios, while the remainder of the men discussed their search and rescue plan. The two groups of two men each entered the woods, while Trooper Cheerman and Grandpa Winfield stepped off the 100 or so paces to the shade of the big oak tree that stood by the former Winfield house.

CHAPTER 19

HEAR SOMETHING?

"Hey Xav," sprouted Oggie, "it's warmer now."

Xavier rolled over and squinted his eyes a couple times to remove the sleep from his eyes.

"It is?"

"Yea, let's get up." Said Oggie pulling on his pants.

"Xavier sat up and looked around the tent in much the condition of a *stupor*.

"You look out yet?" He asked

"Nope, just woke up a couple minutes ago, thought I heard someone call my name. Must'a been part of my dream. But I'll check," said he, creeping to the tent flaps on his hands and knees and crawling outside.

"WOW! What happened? Xavier, come look!" Oggie shouted.

Xavier jumped out of the bed and rustled his pants on, then quickly crawled to the opening and got outside.

"Critters!" Said he with a tinge of disgust in his voice.

"What kind?" Asked Oggie.

Rubbing his eyes to work out the sleep, Xavier headed toward the water and turning his head toward his right shoulder while continuing his stride.

"Probably raccoons." Xavier responded.

At the waters edge, Xavier knelt down and washed his face and eyes thoroughly. Much unlike his counterpart, Xavier was a stickler for procedure and detail. He pulled his T-shirt off and dried his face, then turned toward the tent and gear and proceeded up the short incline from the waters edge to his friends' investigation, slipped inside the tent, retrieved his eyeglasses, cleaned them and put them on, then crawled back outside.

"Oh man look!" Perked Oggie with a disgruntled tilt to his voice, as he held up a half full torn bag of marshmallows.

"Whatever it was got a bunch of stuff."

Catching site of their torn gear, Xavier's face screwed up.

"Hey, this was no raccoon!"

"What?"

"A coon can tear open a marshmallow bag and the bread bag, but I don't think that they can tear this canvas bag," said he holding up a small khaki green bag, which in earlier years had held a gas mask during the Second World War.

"Wow! What'd 'ya think it was."

"Dogs, foxes, or maybe - - a BEAR!"

The boys looked at each other with a startled, wide-eyed look, and almost together in unison responded, "Naw. Couldn't be."

They shook their heads and agreed it hadn't been a bear, or else there would had been prints in the clay like sand. However, secretly, Xavier knew that had there been prints, they would more than likely had been erased by the hard rain he recalled from the night spray. He pondered, 'had that been what had awoken him?' He feared the thought considering that he had simply rolled over and went back to sleep, when he had been pleased at how the rain just seemed to top of the sleep. However, he gazed around the edge of the woods outside their immediate camp area, looking for prints just in case, while Oggie started the task of cleaning up. Not wanting to think upon the idea that a bear had actually visited them last night.

"Let's go hiking now then come back later to clean up the camp and swim." Xavier exclaimed.

"I'm hungry first," said Oggie lifting a marshmallow and tucking it neatly into the cavern known as his mouth that watered for the taste of something sweet.

"Spit it out!" Blurted Xavier, waving his hands wildly at Oggie in a spewing out from the mouth type motion. "Spit it out! Quick!"

Oggie responded in a heartbeat spewing the marshmallow parts all over.

"What is it?" Asked he.

"If it was raccoons, they can carry rabies. Quick, go rinse your mouth out in the pond."

Oggie spit profusely making the most awful regurgitating sounds, the kind that cause even a spectator to gag. The spray of marshmallows went all over their gear and campsite, as Oggie ran to the pond, knelt quickly and cupped his hands in the water and slurped gads of water, gurgling and spitting profusely. Eventually he twisted his rounder and slightly more cumbersome than normal body around to look at Xaiver.

"You don't think I got any of it do 'ya?" He asked.

"No. I don't think so. But, if the marshmallows are carriers then it's everywhere. How ignorant! Why didn't ya' turn your head to spit brainless."

"I guess - - well, er, - - I - -guess I didn't think."

"You never think. Let's put all the opened stuff in a pile and burn it."

"But, what about these marshmallows way down in the bag? I bet they didn't even get touched?" Oggie said, almost pleading for approval to consume them.

"Go ahead. But, don't come slobbering on me if you get rabies and your brain starts swelling inside your skull till you go mad."

Oggie's mouth cringed at the idea while shaking his jaw back and forth then dropped the bag and moved it away with a stick. He then rummaged through one of the camping packs to get his toothbrush and toothpaste. Upon collecting them, he ran to the pond, got his toothbrush wet in the water and preceded to brush his teeth rigorously, occasionally gargling with the toothpaste foam. Oggie stood and turned his head abruptly when he heard his friend Xavier chuckling.

Now looking at Xavier, and with his mouth full of toothpaste foam, Oggie mustered out a barely audible word.

"What?" Doing so, Oggie slobbered some of the toothpaste down the front of his white tee shirt and stepped back leaning his head forward to prevent further reoccurrence.

Xavier laughed and tried to get out the words.

"I don't believe it."

"What?" Asked Oggie sloshing the foam around in his mouth and through his teeth.

"You actually thought to brush your teeth to kill the germs without having to be told. I don't believe it."

Oggie spit the foam out of his mouth.

"OH SHUT UP!" He shouted.

Xavier continued to use a stick to pick up the spoiled goods and packed twigs and sticks around them. They had lost their bread, marshmallows, cookies, and bologna to the intruders. As soon as Oggie was finished rinsing out his mouth, the boys tried to set fire to the pile, but the matches had gotten wet and wouldn't even as much as produce a strike.

"Guess we'll have to let them dry out first," said Oggie.

"Do you think so brilliant?" Mocked Xavier.

"Oh, quit it Xav. How could I know that the marshmallows could have rabies? Besides, I'm hungry."

"Yea, me too," added Xavier picking up a can of mixed vegetables, but I'm not in a mood for vegetables, and besides, we have no fire."

"Yea. So what'll we do?"

Xavier thought for a moment.

"Berries! Let's pack up and go on the hunt of berries, then when we get back, the matches will be dried out and we can heat some other food." He spouted.

"Yea!" Said Oggie.

The boys packed up some backpacks, took a swig of the water from the formerly horrible smelling canteen that now was sweet after washing the canteen thoroughly with bleach water and letting it soak all afternoon with water and baking soda.

"I can't believe this I'm actually drinking out of this canteen," smiled Oggie.

"Yeah, amazing what a little bleach and then baking soda can do? Glad grandma knew that remedy."

The boys threw most of their gear inside the tent to avoid further advertising of their goods to the forest creatures and although Xavier did think last night about tying everything to a rope and then hoist the rope up over a limb in a nearby tree, so that the perishables would be out of the reach of animals; however, upon searching their gear he had discovered that the rope wasn't among the items packed and upon reviewing the list, discovered that neither was it on the list of items to pack, even though they had discussed it. After securing the campsite the adventurer comrades headed off for the days adventure.

Xavier led the way through the woods behind the tent that ushered them to a cliff overlooking a big valley below; this cliff being the same cliff Xavier had spoken of the night before.

"This is where you were headed last night, Og," said Xavier.

Oggie inched to the edge of the cliff carefully with his feet almost sideways and taking baby steps, stretching his head and neck to look down the side of the cliff, then outward at the immense valley that spread out before them below.

"Wow, that's a long way down! And what a view"

"You bet; maybe forty feet or so. Come on let's go around this way," said Xavier pointing to their left, "it doesn't look so steep down that side of the hill."

The cliff was of yellow, tan, and reddish brown sandstone protruding out of the side of the sandy clay hill majestically against the mid-morning sun and the direction in which they were now headed was part of the last mining area where Chief Malcum had been earlier that morning when the boys had heard his voice echoing against the cliff. In fact, when they came to the area where the cliff mated up with the hillside and where they could climb down the steep hillside to the valley below, they were within 400 to 500 yards of that same last mining site area. It was here, about half way down the hill that Oggie stopped, tilted his head, and listened.

"I thought I heard a voice calling," said Oggie. Xavier stopped and listened also. While they listened intently, the breeze rustled the trees almost continually. The voice that Oggie thought he had heard had been the voice of either Chief Malcum or one of the State Policemen who were searching the forest for the boys and had reached the big open more recent strip mine area that was the last mined. Now just separated by a hillside on the Chief's mining side, the 300 to 400 yards of forestation of the un-mined area between that newest mining area and the hillside of the older mining area where Xavier and Oggie now were, the voices even though relatively close, were muffled nearly inaudible let alone the wind rustling the trees covering even that which was audible. Moreover, because Grandpa Winfield had incorrectly stated that the road to the old mining area had been before the dynamite building, Chief Malcum and the others had resultantly been searching in the wrong area, an error that at that moment prevented Xavier and Oggie's rescue and would place them at greater risk for what was to come.

"Guess I was just hearing things," said Oggie.

"May have been the wind," said Xavier, "c'mon let's go."

The boys started down over the hill which would further the difficulty of hearing the rescue teams voices.

"Remember this cliff. Our camp is just beyond it," said Xavier giving Oggie some direction.

Oggie looked to his right while scaling down the steep terrain. "But it goes around the other direction where we can't see the other end. So, how will we know exactly where our camp is?"

Xavier stopped and looked to where the cliff curved around the far right of them out of vision, then looked back to where they had scaled down the hillside at the point where the cliff ended into the steep hillside.

"Well - - just remember that we came down on the right side of the cliff."

"Oh yea," replied Oggie. And with that settled, the boys continued down the remainder of the incline to the level valley.

CHAPTER 20

WHERE ARE THEY?

Meanwhile, back at the strip mine entrance area the search team had now congregated near the old farmhouse area to meet up with Grandpa Winfield; then, regroup their search efforts had the first wave proved unsuccessful, as it did of course. When the search group arrived at destination, Grandpa and Grandma Winfield were waiting with food and drinks to refresh the team. Mrs. Bartholomew ran to her husband. As he embraced her, he began explaining the results of their search thus far through panting breaths, and how the rain had simply removed any sign of the boys' whereabouts.

"You gonna be all right?" Asked Mrs. Bartholomew noticing how her husband was breathing hard..

"Guess I've gotten a little outta shape," replied he with a chuckle, vowing to himself earlier that once this was over he and Oggie would be doing hikes together because he needed to spend more time with Oggie and he desperately needed the exercise.

"Sure do appreciate you men doing this," praised Mr. Winfield handing Chief Malcum a soda pop.

"No problem Mr. Winfield," responded Chief Malcum, "thanks to you Mrs. Winfield and Mrs. Bartholomew for the food and drinks." Chief Malcum reached for the bottle opener, opened the bottle, and quickly slurped down a first gulp to quench his ailing thirst from nearly five hours of searching.

"Your welcome," replied the ladies. Chief Malcum proceeded to introduce the State Police officers as the food and drinks were being distributed. The officers were thanked for their assistance, by the parents and guardians but other than Grandpa Winfield, the others did not know that the real reason for the State Police participation was of course deeper driven. For not only were they on the search for the missing boys, but also the potential escaped criminals, who just might be in these woods.

"Now Mr. Winfield, tell me where else in these woods you might expect these explorers to traipse off to," asked Malcum as if it were really an order as he laid out the map on the back of the car and pointed out the areas already searched.

"Well, if they weren't at the deep ditch strip mine then I'd expect -" continued Grandpa Winfield pointing to the map, "Then they must be here."

Harold Winfield proceeded to tell and point out to Chief Malcum and the others about the older mining areas on the left of the main trail up the roadbed about 300 to 600 yards from the entrance area where they now stood, but whose road had been removed. He then explained more about the older roadway that was near the dynamite building and how to find this trail with the aid of a spring landmark, the same spring which Xavier and Oggie had drank out of the day before. Lastly, he further explained those first sites on the right at about the same distance as the deep ditch site, but whose lead road entrance was hidden by the underbrush just before the abandoned dynamite building, again giving the wrong location of the entrance. The search team recalled the dynamite building but no recollection of anything resembling a roadbed. Grandpa resounded the directions, but again he gave an incorrect location for the entrance, for it had been many years since he had made the trip that far into these woods.

Had Harold Winfield given the correct directions, perhaps the outcome would have been different. Chief Malcum explained how he had to make his rounds then take his wife to the doctor and could resume the search at 2:00 pm.

CHAPTER 21

THAT SMELL

"Look!" Shouted Xavier sprinting off in a run toward a large area of thick growth.

"What is it?" Queried Oggie picking up the pace to join the pace of his pal.

"Berries!"

"Wow! Great! Look how many!"

The boys had gotten to the foot of the hill and were deep in a valley of crab apple and locust trees. Being the very first of the mining areas, this un-reclaimed area was marshy with some eroded high ground that passed though the center almost like a road. Moreover, along the lower side of the high ground upon which the boys walked was a peppering of dense patches of blackberries and red raspberries.

"Let's eat up, Og."

"You got it pal," said Oggie skipping down off the high ground to encapsulate himself with the nectar of the land.

The boys ate berries for the better part of two hours continuing along the high ground in the same direction that they had been going moving deeper into this densely vegetated area. Exchanging conversation about their excursion thus far including the rain last night and their late night visitors, proved to alarm them to begin looking around cautiously.

"Where's the cliff?" Asked Oggie looking around.

Xavier poked his head out of the berry bushes for a moment.

"Ouch!" He exclaimed.

"What happened?" Asked Oggie.

"Got stuck again. That's maybe eight or nine times now." Xavier sucked his thumb where the prickly point of the berry bushes had penetrated his skin, while wading through the high brush to the road like higher ground. He looked around and couldn't find the cliff. Seeing a large hump of ground just ahead, he walked over and up on it. Oggie waded up out of the brush to the high ground also.

"There it is," said Xavier looking back in the direction in which they had ascended from.

"I can barely see the top of the cliff over top all these crab apple trees."

As Oggie joined him he tiptoed and stretched a gaze in the direction of Xavier's view, "I can't see it."

"Tip toe and look where I'm pointing." Xavier pointed in the direction of the cliff then grabbed Oggie by the waist and helped lift him up some, since Xavier was nearly a head's height over his friend, and thus he reasoned that Oggie might need some assistance.

"Wow! It sure is far away," said the shorter but heavier Oggie.

"Yer eatin' too many berries," said Xavier dropping his lift.

"I mean -- I could almost lift ya' easy last year, but not now."

"It's cause I'm 10 now," said Oggie in his defense. "When you get older you get bigger and heavier."

"Pew!" Xavier exclaimed.

"What is it?" Asked Oggie.

"You let one or what?"

"No!"

"Smell!" Exclaimed Xavier snarling his nose.

Oggie took in a slow deep draw of air through his nose, placing special attention to what he smelled.

"Yuck," said he, "what is it?"

Xavier moved around following his scent, "I don't know, but it sure does stink."

"Yea," said Oggie looking around on both sides of the long path of high ground upon which they now stood. It was as though this were some old abandoned road that had grown up. It was in fact, the entrance to this abandoned strip mine some 30 years earlier, the other end of which lead out to Lake Road, a road that ran adjacent to a nearby county lake that also happened to be the source of the town's water supply.

"It's stronger over this way," said Xavier sniffing and snubbing his nose in the direction along the roadbed away from the cliff.

As the day had heated up, the wind had just recently died down so that the smell just sort of hung around in areas of concentrated stronger smell and diluted weaker smells. Xavier's logic began to kick in as he held up his red handkerchief as if it were a flag, to discern the direction of the light occasional breeze. With such a light breeze now, discernment was difficult, however, he continued his search in the direction of the occasional breeze while carefully sniffing to check the strength of the aroma. 'Clearly it was something dead,' he reasoned, 'and judging from the strength of the scent, maybe large.' Oggie followed close in the direction of Xavier's search looking high and low for the origin of the odor.

"We're getting close," said Xavier motioning his hand and pointing his finger forward and to the left of their present position. Oggie perked up a few quick paces to side with his partner, then a few extra steps forward to take the lead. The scent was strong enough to gag. At the side of the roadbed, the ground dropped off with a bank, so the boys moved down the grade carefully. In the ravine along the roadway, the smell just kind of hung there, low and overtook the shorter and less stomach strong of the two. Oggie bent over and gagged, it was a dry heave type gag; but, a gag nonetheless.

"Eeee gads this is getting to me," said he stretching his head and neck upward to gaze at Xaiver. Oggie was turning pale. Xavier was mirroring Oggie's action. The air was dry and cool, but be it the hot sun on his back or his weakness from the gagging, standing there with his hands on his knees the sickness was from the smell and was getting the best of him and he instantly broke out into a profuse sweat and needed to lay down.

This gagging reflected on to Xavier who watched his buddy and mimicked several gags with him. As Oggie regained his composure and lifted his body erect to stand up straight, his eyes focused forward to an area where the high grass was all smashed down about 10 to 12 feet away. Then, like a bolt of lightning it hit him like being smacked by an eighteen-wheeler truck.

CHAPTER 22

LET'S GET OUTTA HERE!

"Ahhhhhhh! Ahhhhhhh!" Screamed Oggie in place dancing his legs up and down in a low stepped pace as if he were running in place.

About thirty feet down the bank ahead of them was the carcass of a large dead animal with internal organs and guts strewn everywhere, the wide midsection of which was covered extensively with large amounts of blood, that painted the ground in a ghastly dark red. The site was appalling and most horrific; actually, totally frightening.

"Ahhhh!!! Ahhhhhh!" Screamed he again; and again, "Ahhhhhh!!"

Close behind, Xavier stepped quickly forward the few steps to end up behind Oggie fighting the anxious steps of his frightened friend to see. As Xavier's heart raced, he thought, 'What on earth was it!' Unable to see around Oggie, he hollered out to him.

"What is it!" Which fueled the fire of Oggie's scream.

"Ahhhh! Ahhhh!!" Exclaimed Oggie screaming and turning quickly and trying desperately to gain a footing on the steep bank of the road ground that he had descended earlier.

"Run! It's awful! Run!" Screamed he as he pushed against the shocked and standing in place Xavier, who also was trying to see the ghastly mess. The push against Xavier's chest coupled with the poor footing of the hillside, the two boys fell, one atop the other. They fought to both get off each other and in particular Oggie fought to be free of this ghastly area.

"What is it?" Inquired Xavier again, as Oggie climbed over Xavier, stepping on his chest in the rush.

"It's dead! Run!" Oggie fought to be free, but his limbs seemed to be useless against the gravity of the hillside and the clawing of Xavier to get free of his friends' frantic moves.

"I don't know," said he shaking his head back and forth, "it's all over the place."

Xavier took hold of Oggie's shoulders and rolled him to one side, shaking him back and forth.

"HEY!! Get Hold!!" Xavier screamed directly at Oggie.

Oggie looked straight ahead connecting eyes with Xavier while he tried to regain his composure from the rush of the hysteria.

"It's awful Xav! I mean totally awful!" Yelled back Oggie with a pitiful disturbed expression and looking like he was about to cry from fear and anxiety.

"I see it!" Said Xavier turning to look at the tragedy below them in the weeds. As the awful site burned into Xavier's memory, and on almost the same cue, the boys turned, sprang into motion, and scurried the incline to the top of the roadbed where Oggie leaned forward with hands on knees and regurgitated profusely.

"For cryin' out loud," remarked Xavier holding back his own gag.

"I can't help it!" Said Oggie wiping his mouth clean with his large red handkerchief.

"That's sick." Xavier turned his head and dry gagged a couple times.

Feeling a little insecure at the moment and weak from the visual trauma, Xavier easily convinced Oggie that they should go back to the camp.

"By now the matches should be dried out and we can start a fire." Xaiver tried to change the subject, while also, clearing his own mind of the awfulness that they just witnessed.

Oggie on the other hand, tried desperately to convince Xavier that they should go home since their food rations had been destroyed by the intruders. In addition, deep down inside he was still quite fearful of the thoughts of night fall again and having to spend another night in the woods, especially in light of whatever it was that had mangled and dismembered that poor animal.

"What do you think it was?" Asked Oggie.

"A deer," said Xavier looking at his pal Oggie as they continued a steady pace back in the direction of the cliff that would lead them to their camp.

"A deer can do something like that!" Exclaimed Oggie, his facial muscles forcing his forehead and ears back in amazement.

"No stupid!" Said Xavier shaking his head back and forth left and right in short strokes. "I think it was a deer that was killed."

"Hey, I'm not stupid!"

"Really?" Asked Xavier stopping his stride as if it were a confirming statement. "Then why'd ya ask such a silly question?"

Stopping a few steps ahead of Xavier, Oggie swiveled his step to look back at his taller life long buddy.

"Well, then what do you think did it?" Challenged Oggie.

"I don't know," responded Xavier, "what difference does it make anyway?"

Still feeling uneasy from the dreadful site that he could not erase or extinguish from his memory, Xavier placed his hands on his hip and scolded his shorter friend.

"Well, did you stop to think that that mess could be you?"

"No way!" Shouted back Oggie in his defense, "I tole ya, I'm goin' home!" Having said that, Oggie disconnected their stare then turned and re-established the pace in the direction of the cliff.

"Really?" Inquired Xavier, still standing in the same spot.

"Yea!" Shouted Oggie back over his shoulder with his head high in pride for having made a good decision for a change, at least to his estimation anyway.

Running a few quick steps to side up with his partner, Xavier poked his head in front of Oggie.

"Well what if the thing that did that is at our camp right now?"

Oggie pushed Xavier back with his left hand.

"Quit it!" Oggie walked only a few more steps then stopped dead in his tracks and spun around in haste.

"Do you think it is?"

"Sure, but don't you suppose it'd be afraid of us?"

"Don' know." Oggie tilted his head and thought for a second or two, "I suppose. It's what my dad says anyway."

"Yea, mine too," agreed Xavier, "but do ya think they ever ran into something like what did that?" Oggie frowned with his mouth and shook his head back and forth then shrugged his shoulders placing credence to Xavier's *supposition*.

While standing there, just ahead the boys heard rustling in the bushes slightly below them and off to their right. Their wide eyes stared hard holes through each other as chills ran up their spines. Their raised eyebrows certified that neither of them had any idea as to the exact origin or nature of the rustled noise. Nor, did they have any desire at the moment to know of its' extent. However, Xavier's wit slowly dismissed the fear that was trying to take control. Moreover, though their brief exposure to the rustling bush served only to ignite more fear even deep inside to their very souls, Xavier began to think.

The seconds began to seem like hours as their senses awakened to capture even the slightest movement or sound wave.

Both boys looked around carefully. Xavier held his finger at his mouth to silence Oggie while they each began to visually survey every tree and even water puddles from last nights rain for footprints or any kind of mark that would give a clue as to the identity of the creature that did this awful thing.

"We gotta get hold," whispered Xavier, as the two forcefully challenged their adrenaline to focus on reality. Their breathing had increased and their hearts pounding, filling their ears with an unavoidable throbbing fear.

Xaviers' thoughts were focused upon the fact that the dried blood on the dead animal indicated a kill from a few days ago. And the damage to their camping gear was unequivocally caused by no small animal. 'Therefore,' concluded he, 'it must be their most dreaded fear.....a BEAR!' The energy in his nervous system vibrated and overflowed so loudly he could not hear his friend Oggie whispering that the bush rustler was on the move.

"Xavier," whispered Oggie a second time and pushing at Xaviers' chest with his left arm, "Xavier."

Xavier broke his thought long enough to recognize his friends action.

"What?"

"It's on the move." Oggie pointed in the direction where he had last heard the rustled bushes. Xavier looked and not seeing anything asked with a whisper.

"What?" He whispered back.

"I heard it moving."

"Where?"

Oggie pointed at the same spot he had pointed to earlier. While Oggie's eyes were dead focused on the spot where he had last heard the rustling, Xavier's eyes looked to the left, right, and beyond that spot; for if the thing were on the move, then more than likely it would not be in the same spot as earlier.

"There!" Xavier whispered loudly pointing to the tops of a leafy bush that shook for only a second or two.

"I tole ya, Xav," whispered Oggie scooting a little closer to Xavier and moving his left arm close enough to touch Xavier's side. He felt better to know how close his friend was for he reasoned that when two are closer there is some strength in numbers that drives up the level of ones' confidence and security. Feeling a little more comfortable, Oggie spoke quietly.

"What is it?"

Disgusted with his own lack of knowledge in this whole matter, and feeling the beginning stages of frustration for how this camping trip was going, Xavier frowned.

"How should I know?" Xavier touted.

"Well, you always do."

Whatever it was, the thing was moving away from the roadway that the boys were standing on, and that pleased Xavier very much.

"Let's go," whispered Xavier pointing toward the cliff and starting to tiptoe quietly and slowly in the direction of the cliff along the old roadbed, "but be quiet."

"Is it safe?" Asked Oggie.

Xavier didn't want Oggie to know that even he had no idea at this point of what was safe or not safe and certainly didn't want to place any undue fear in his lifelong friend. However, beyond a shadow of a doubt, concerned he was for the knowledge of what it was that was rustling the bush too near them as far as he was concerned. Moreover, the direction of the intruder seemed to have been perpendicular to the general direction of their camp, though they could no longer see or hear any movement at all at that very instant.

"Oggie, look," pointed Xavier quietly toward the cliff over which sat their camp some 1,000 feet or so. Oggie tiptoed and turned his head a little to the left where Xavier visually directed. Meanwhile, Xaiver scanned the right side of the roadway for movement.

"Oh yea," responded Oggie with a whisper back, "It's the cliff. Hey, what say we climb it?"

"Are you crazy, it's almost straight up."

"No it's not. See there," said he pointing to an area where the erosion had carved out an indentation along the straight wall, making for a steep climb, but perhaps maneuverable.

"Maybe." Xavier saw nothing and quickly gave in to Oggie's suggestion. Besides, it sounded like a great experience; and, it would get them away from where they were.

CHAPTER 23

CLIMBING ANYONE?

So, the boys continued cautiously along the roadway to the point where the roadbed headed up the steep incline into the woods where they had been earlier when they first came to this area. Having left the roadbed and moving along the base of the cliff to the left they stepped over fallen rocks and around boulders. Xavier had looked back occasionally over this shoulder and upon seeing no further movement or suspicious sounds was certain that whatever they had encountered moments ago had gone further to the right of the roadbed and was now far gone.

Reaching the *alcove* in the side of the hillside, they stopped and looked up the sides of the cliff and the steep incline, now appraising whether or not they could ascend it. In the short, they decided to attempt the climb.

"See. I tole 'ya we could climb it," said Oggie forcing his mouth corners and cheeks high to produce a fake frown much like that of a clown.

"Hey that looks good on 'ya," sneered Xavier briefly placing his thumbs in his ears with his fingers pointing up in the air and wiggling them profusely; while also, sticking his tongue out. After this brief mock he lowered his arms and continued climbing,

"What if your face froze like that? I've heard of it happening." Laughed Xavier.

Waving off Xavier in disbelief and starting up the incline of fallen clay earth and rocks, Oggie prepared to make a statement with confidence.

"You're full of it Xav."

"Oh yeah. Well, I have."

Oggie stopped climbing the incline and looked down at his friend.

"Yea right." It was both a statement and question.

"Really. I mean it."

"Oh yeah. Who?"

"I don't really remember exactly, it was this guy who invented something though."

"Really. What'd he invent, freezers or ice or something like that?"

"No I remember! It was a guy by the name of Frost."

"Oh yeah, Xav. What'd they do; name frost after him?"

"Yea, in fact, they did. He was out too long one day and made this frown at somebody and it froze like that. And people went around saying, 'that it's as cold as old Frost's face,' and so they named ice on the ground in the mornings after him."

"Really? If so, what's his first name?"

Xavier tilted his head and closed his eyes while peeking slightly to see if Oggie was still looking.

"I.... I...think it was John or Jake maybe. No! It was Jack. Jack Frost." Xavier said nodding his head. "Yeah that's it, Jack Frost."

"Hey, I've heard my mom talk about Jack Frost. Where'd he live?"

"Right here in Chestnut Ridge I think."

Oggie stepped off a few paces down the incline closer to Xavier.

"How'd his face freeze anyways?" Oggie inquired.

Xavier held back a grin, "He was like making fun of someone and was eating this like really cold Popsicle and made a frown and it like froze."

"Really? How do you suppose that happened?"

Xavier looked up the incline and started stepping forward. Oggie's eyes and face followed Xavier's movements.

"Well, Og... it was probably because ole Jack was the kind of guy that was just about as gullible as you." Xavier laughed silently inside.

Oggie stood still for a moment thinking and pondering his friends' trickery as Xavier started up the incline past him. Moving quickly, Oggie stepped a few quick paces up the hillside and grabbed Xaviers' right ankle and pulled. Xavier fell quickly and started sliding down the hillside, sliding right under Oggie and sending the two boys tumbling down the incline of the hillside with a rush of dust and tumbling pebbles following.

"Way ta' go numskull," scoffed Xavier getting up spitting out sand and dust, then brushing the dust from his jeans and shirt.

"Well, deserves ya right for kiddin' me."

"Yea. Sometimes you amaze me. I mean, Jack Frost? C'mon." Xavier chuckled a couple times which prompted Oggie to quickly push against Xavier's chest, causing him to fall backwards over a small boulder about knee high. Xaiver tumbled over and landed on his back.

"Oh shut up!" Hollered Oggie.

"O.K. Fair play," gave in Xavier to a fair game trickery and payback.

And with that the two boys once again began their ascent. About half way up the hill, the incline became much steeper than it appeared at the foot of the hill. Moreover, the earthen soil was loose in some places preventing a good footing.

"Like this," instructed Xavier, using his leg to pound the heel of his tennis shoes against the soil to create a step. "See, then you can step in 'em."

Oggie observed and followed the pattern of his friend until they reached the rock cliff that seemed to protrude the hillside for yet another twenty feet or so from the top ledge.

"Xav. It's a long way down."

"You think so?" Mocked Xavier.

"Yea. What if one of us fell?"

"What if?"

"I mean, you know we could like fall."

Both boys stopped and held their positions by forcing their legs and arms against rocks and molded dirt steps they had just made, then looked back down the hill and observed a huge boulder at the foot of the incline which would become a stopping point, were they to fall.

"Hum!" Discouraged Xavier. "That boulders positioned nicely to stop us."

Looking down Oggie replied with as much a statement as a question, "Yeah, but wouldn't we like smash against it?"

"Oh no," smirked Xavier, "it'd cushion our fall."

Oggie looked up to see Xavier shaking his head back and forth in disbelief.

"Well, I was just saying it for cryin' out loud." Oggie defended.

"It goes without saying Og. It's like looking at a dead person and saying, 'he looks nice' but in reality he's dead. I mean, you don't have to say he's dead, it's recognized. Know what I mean."

"Oh shut up Xav, what'er we gonna do?"

"Well, since it was your bright idea to climb this thing, why don't you tell us."

"Well, er..."

"Yeah. Well?"

The two looked up above them and discussed trying to descend the hill believing that their further ascent might be too treacherous. And although at the base of the cliff, the incline seemed manageable, from where they presently were the incline had sharpened its' ascent and some of the rocks which they had just stepped from, broke loose and rolled down the hillside, the rolling rock crashing into pieces as they struck the big boulder at the rock cliff base.

"We just gotta do it," assured Xavier.

"But we're gonna fall for sure, Xav?" Pleaded Oggie, his legs now getting weak.

"Look, if we try to go down, we'll fall for sure. Half the rocks we were climbing on broke loose and fell. And besides, we can't see our footing below us very well, but the footing at our eye level and at our body level is easy to see. We just have to be smart."

"Maybe smart would be to slide down."

"Yea right dummy. And then tumble head over heels into that big monster at the bottom."

Xavier noticed that there was a rock ledge above them and off to their right if only they could ascend about three or four feet. But, there didn't appear to be any footing there.

"Boost me, Og. I see a landing on top this rock."

"How am I gonna boost ya, when I'm about ready to fall right now myself."

"Pound and dig your feet in a step above where you are now and when I'm ready push on my feet. Then I'll pull you up."

Oggie did so as Xavier instructed and when the moment came for the push, he held on to a rock ledge on his left and with his right hand placed under Xavier's right foot. As Oggie pushed, Xavier stretched to reach the ledge with his hands. Then, just as Oggie was losing footing with his right foot, Xavier grasp a lip on the edge of the rock cliff ledge and began pulling himself up.

"HELP!!! Xavier!! Help!" Oggie's right footing gave way causing him to swing across the rock opening to the right. Just as he was about to fall, he grasp a protruding flat stone with both hands allowing him to hold his position with one foot firm on a jagged rock on the left side of the ravine and both his hands on that flat stone across on the right. This awkward position resulted in him being suspended with one foot on a rock, his hands on a flat stone on the right and his right foot dangling loose. He tried several times to get a footing somewhere on the hillside with his right foot, but attempts to do so seemed to lessen his grasp on the flat rock ledge, so he stopped trying and hollered.

"Help Xav!!" Xavier had disappeared above him.

"Where ya at?" Xavier responded on his hands and knees leaning over the rock ledge that he had just accomplished.

"I'm gonna fall! Hurry!"

Xavier could see his pal hanging on for dear life.

"Hold on a sec."

"Hurry!" Oggie's voice was trembling and shaky.

Xavier looked below Oggie and from this much better viewpoint, he realized that if his little buddy were to fall it would be certain that he would be hurt seriously or even worse: fatal. The height was even making Xavier light headed. Quickly he refocused his thoughts from thinking about the conditions to thinking about survival and solutions. Many options raced through his head. If he were to attempt a climb down, one or both would lose their footings respectively and he and his friend would fall for sure and tumble to the distance far below where the large boulder awaited their arrival to cause some serious human damage. 'What could he do?'

Just then he looked behind and above him. He was but a toss to the top and it was an easy climb. 'A branch,' he thought, 'Or better, a grapevine.' He'd remember seeing several of them.

"Hold on Og, I got an idea!"

"Hurry Xav. I can't hold much longer. My arms are getting tired." His friends voice was weak, indicative of effort and inability to get a deep breath.

Xavier quickly shot up the dirt slope above the rock ledge sending down sandy clay and pebbles over Oggie. Xavier surfaced at the grassy ledge and thought about the exact direction of the camp, and remembered seeing a brown downed tree and grape vine. Quickly he scurried to the vine and untangled its' hold against the tree which had formerly life supported the vine before falling. Even as the boy fought to untangle the vine from the fallen tree he was reminded of how stupid a grape vine must be. After all, the vine had obviously choked out the trees life support system, with its' own leaves, by climbing the host, which is the tree, then sprouting out its' own leaves covering the trees own leaves, and then the tree dies bringing down both the tree and the vine that killed it. 'So,' he had thought, 'grape vines were suicidal.' But fortunate for them this vines suicidal mission was in a perfect position to allow just enough of the untangled vine rope to pull to the edge of the rock cliff and lower it down to Oggie.

"Here grab hold!" Yelled down Xavier as he lured down the vine rope near Oggie's body, accidentally striking him in the head.

"Hey man, you tryin' to kill me?"

"Try to spread your arms and I'll lower it between them. Then, grab hold!" From the rock cliff edge, Xavier climbed down to the slightly lower landing then lifted the vine carefully and lowered it between Oggie's arms. The young lad loosened his grip with one hand and reached for the vine but missed. The jerk of his body caused his footing to slip and he started to roll out away from the hillside. Xavier gasped. 'God help us!' He pleaded mentally, 'Please God?' As the shaking young lads only foot hold lost its' balance, the protruded flat rock that he was standing on, broke loose, causing Oggie to slip downward fast but with his one hand free he quickly grasp the hanging vine. Lightning fast, especially for Oggie, his other hand reached for and grasped the vine. It wasn't a good hold, but it was a decent enough one to support him for the moment. With a thud, the little boys body smashed against the hillside. Xavier listened as the falling rock, dirt, and debris rushed down the hillside. He could not tell if his friend were part of the falling objects. 'Please God help us!' Xavier again cried internally with all of his inner being, listening carefully while hoping and praying.

"Ugh." Came the sullen sound against the cliff wall.

"You O.K.?" Xavier could hardly see his pal. Right where Oggie was hanging was a slight protrusion of dirt and rock. The young lad hung there suspended against the side of the rocky hillside. He was safe.

"I can't breathe," came a mushy whisper.

"Hold on." Xavier closed his eyes for just an instant and prayed, 'Please Lord, don't let him fall. Please give him strength.' Even though fearful thoughts raced through his mind, he confirmed his prayer, 'Oggie just has to make it!'

"Xav," the voice was a little stronger, "I can't hold on."

"Don't move Og, just hold on!" Xavier sat down over top the vine where it hung over the edge.

"Hold on tight Oggie, I'll try to pull you up." Xavier knew that this was fruitless. How on earth could his skinny lightweight frame hoist his much heavier friend. 'Help me Lord!' He whispered in his head as he grabbed the vine just as he did in those gym classes at school during those 'tug 'o war' exercises where he always did lousy.

"I can't hold on Xav!" Oggie's voice was stronger, evidence that he had gotten his breath back.

"Lift yourself a little and wrap your legs around the vine!" The vine jerked back and forth giving evidence to Oggie's attempts to firm his grip.

"You ready?"

"Don't let go Xav. Please don't let go!" Oggie was now placing all of his safety, life, and faith in the hands of his best friend.

Even though he knew it were impossible, Xavier leaned forward, grabbed the vine, and shure'd up his footing against the dirt hillside, sending some of the loose soil over the edge.

"Hey, watch it! What'ya doin'?"

"Hold on and don't waste your energy talking."

Xaiver pulled the first pull and it was like dead weight, not even a budge; again he grasp the vine and pulled with everything he had and still no budge. In fact, he was sure that with the last pull the vine might have slipped an inch.

'Please God give me the strength,' he whispered to himself as he prepared to pull a third time. Having expended all the energy he had in the previous two pulls he was certain that his weakened muscles would not pull his friend Oggie from the tragedy that awaited him. For the first time in Xavier's life he was totally saddened and wanted to cry but knew he must remain strong for his friend below him.

Then, he took a deep breath, looked upward into the heavens, closed his eyes, and whispered, 'I'm finished God, I have nothing left, its totally up to you. Please help us!' He grasped the vine rope, squeezed it, and pulled knowing that his efforts were fruitless. The vine pulled up an inch or so. He was sure of it, but couldn't believe it. Once again, Xavier squeezed, then pulled again, except with what felt like a little harder this time and with strength that he was sure he didn't have, Xavier could feel the veins in his head pressing outward from the strain he was exerting; again, an inch, maybe even two. Who was counting? Another pull, exerting even more pull power over the last with his digging in deeper, pushing more loose soil over the hill; however, no comments from below. 'Perhaps his friend was listening to what he had told him and was actually being quite and pulling or had somehow passed out but then how could he still be holding onto the vine,' he questioned and thought. Nonetheless, Xavier knew Oggie had to be there and just did what he knew he had to do at this point: pull.

The vine widened just a little where he gripped for the next pull and somehow the pull was easier. Xavier smiled inside, he knew these pulls were not his, because before he began this exercise he had been expended of all his energy, yet somehow, someone, was helping him accomplish the impossible, he was lifting a dead weight that was heavier than he was while also in a very awkward position. He smiled and pulled again and wanted to look over his shoulder to see if someone was helping but knew if that had been the case, he would have felt the tugging on the loose vine behind him.

Again and again he pulled, hanging on to the vine with all the hold and pulling force he could source from within and without, steadily inching his one hand in front of the other for another grip and pull. The vine jerked indicative of Oggie's attempt to assist in the hoisting. 'What a challenge,' the young Xaiver thought trying to avoid the pounding fear inside him that wanted to take control, 'what an excursion to remember.' Pulling back as far as he could stretch back, the vine suddenly jerked free causing him to nearly loose his footing while rolling to the side and nearly over the edge.

"Oggie!!! Oggie!!" He screamed at the top of his voice while jerking to gain his footing and gaze over the edge trying to listen for his friend crashing down the hillside.

"What?" Came the response. "What a sight!" There on his side on top the very ledge that Xavier had climbed onto not more than a few minutes ago, was Oggie all covered with dirt and dust.

"Thank you God!" Exclaimed Xavier scurrying to his knees and over to where Oggie lay, seemingly helpless. Reaching his hand forward, Oggie grabbed hold as Xavier excitedly reached out his hand and grabbing Oggie's hand, pulled the heavy little object up the remaining incline distance to safety. They both fell on their backs looking up into the heavens and breathed several deep breaths to help expel the remaining anxiety that had taken both their breaths.

Xavier gazed into the bright blue sky peppered with cotton ball clouds while mentally thanking God for having allowed his buddy to make it. After realizing that there was no way he could have accomplished such a monumental task he thanked God twice more then thought, 'what a story!' After moments of silent reflection, Xavier leaned up on one arm and faced Oggie.

"You O.K.?"

Still lying flat on his back, Oggie rolled his head in the direction of his pal Xavier.

"Hh yea, but what a rush!"

"Rush? You scared me half to death!"

"You? You moron! Who do you think was hanging out there over a valley of death?"

"Moron? After saving your life you call me moron?" Frowned Xavier.

"Well. Sorry." They just sat there looking at each other for what seemed like an hour, but in reality maybe a minute or two.

"That was some hill!" Exclaimed Oggie breaking the pressure of silence.

"Yea, I'll say it was. Last time I listen to you, you horse's butt."

"O.K., we're even." Touted Oggie feeling he had enough strength to lean up on one arm.

"Huh?" Xavier sat full upright now looking at Oggie puzzled by that last comment.

"You called me a horse's rear and I called you moron."

"Oh I see," agreed Xavier sporting a frown with cringed eyebrows and nodding his head.

"Well, now what?"

"To the camp!" Yelled Xavier, "Let's go home."

"Cool man."

The two boys stood up, moving away from the cliffs edge apiece and began dusting themselves and each other off.

"Man you sure got dirty."

"Yea, it's because you were sending half the hill down on me; probably on purpose."

"Yea, I didn't have anything else to do Og."

The boys chuckled and pushed their hands at each other like they were boxing and began to laugh.

"Boy will we have something great to tell our kids Xav."

"I'll say," chuckled Xavier, "The Great Camping Adventure."

"Huh?" Questioned Oggie.

"What we been going through meat head."

They both chuckled and turned toward the woods to head for camp. They entered the woods looking behind them occasionally to see the disappearing cliff's edge. A welcomed site for sure. Just then, right in front of them from behind a large oak tree not more than eight feet away, emerged a large figure with both arms extended in the air.

"AAAhhhhhhh!!!!!!"

CHAPTER 24

AN INTRUDER

The two boys bounced backwards at just a glance of the creature and tripped over each other, falling on their backs rolled on their sides quickly and scrambled to get up. Before they could get up, the thing overtook them with its' arms stretched out in the air like branches on a tree, grabbing at their legs.

"Aaaaahhhhhh!!!!!!" It was large and beastly looking from where they lay.

"We're gonna get killed Xav!" Oggie screamed rolling over and forcing his face into the ground. Xavier tried to see what kind of creature it was but was unable to because of the bright blinding afternoon sun above the figure that stood then knelt above them.

"It's got me!" Oggie screamed louder trying to kick free his now captive right leg.

"Help!!" He cried out in fear while trying to scramble toward the cliff, away from the being that was mangling his leg. In a flash he felt something wrapped around his leg tightly.

"Help, Xavier!! HELP!" Xavier tried to reach for Oggie's leg, but scurried to free his own leg that was being grasped with a lot of force.

"Ouch!" Hollered Xaiver, "that hurts!" He could see a rope wrapped around his ankle. It was a rope tied with a special knot that only got tighter if you tried to pull it loose by any means other than that which would release it. Xavier held his hand up and could see that the figure resembled a man.

Looking closer, it was definitely a man and he was in some kind of special uniform.

"Who are you?" Queried the young Xavier gasping to catch his breath from the sudden attack of excitement.

"And why'd you tie our feet together like that?" Xavier demanded with inquiry.

Oggie on the other hand had broken into a controlled emotional cry.

"Who are you? And, why'd you tie us up?" Asked Oggie, his legs also tied to Xavier with that same special knot.

The large figure backed up a few steps permitting a better view. It was a grown man. He was scruffy looking and dressed in a black and white horizontal striped uniform. He was tall and dark complexioned. Xavier studied the man's movements as he moved backward to a fallen tree and sat upon it. The mans' steps were somewhat unsure and unstable testifying to the witted boy that the man had not been in the woods too often; and, the uniform definitely indicative of a Corrections Department issue. Oggie rolled over and sniffled a few times.

"Oh no! It's a prisoner Xav! We're gonners!" He rolled back over and continued his bawling.

"What do you want with us?" Asked Xavier.

"What you boys doin' here?"

Xavier thought for a moment about what not to say, and before he could respond Oggie spoke out.

"We're just campin', please don't kill us." As the words left Oggie's lips, Xavier frowned.

"Nice. Campin' huh? Well then you boys won't mind showin' me the way to your camp so's I can get me some grub hey?"

"We're camped down in the valley," pointed Xavier toward the cliff.

"Aw, that's a bunch of baloney boy," said the man, "I been here two nights and there ain't been nuttin' in that valley except whatever it was that tore that deer to smithereens. So, fess up."

"We're over there," pointed Oggie over his back in the general direction of where their camp actually was.

"Stand up and show me!" Hollered the man, "Aw'm starved."

"He's wrong," said Xavier pointing toward the cliff and motioning in the direction of where the road and cliff met.

"The camps somewhere over there and we gotta follow a trail."

"You sure? Don't lie ta me boy." The man frowned a powerful scowl that would stop an eight-day clock. Xavier's heart raced fearing what the man might do were he to discover that Xavier's direction would lead them away from the camp and into the newer mining pit which was out of the woods and into the open.

"Yea mister. We gotta follow the trail or we'll get lost in these woods."

"No we don't," said Oggie setting up on his knees and wiping his nose and his tears with his hand.

"Xavier can get us anywhere in here without a trail 'cause his grandpa owns this place."

"That right?" Said the man nodding his head up and down while fixing his eyes on Xavier's eyes. "You lyin' to me boy?"

"No sir," said Oggie fixing a truthful expression upon his face as he turned toward the man.

"Not you mouth," said the man insultingly to Oggie, "your stupid friend."

Xavier's heart raced faster responding a little more cautiously.

"Well, that's true what he said," nodding his head toward Oggie then continuing, "But.... you just got me mixed up with that scare. And besides, comin' up that hill just scared us to death, so I'm a little mixed up right now. That's why it's better to follow the cliff to the road."

Oggie tilted his head at Xavier in amazement. 'What? Xavier not sure of himself?' Thought he.

"Well the road I know," responded the man, "it's how I followed you boys. Thought ya was gonna fall off that hill I did until your friend there saved ya." The man of course was speaking of Xavier's actions to save Oggie earlier.

"What do ya want with us?" Queried Xavier.

"Just none yer business boy, you get me to that camp. Now shut up and move." The man pushed Xavier and Oggie who were tied together by way of that tied knot to each other's closest ankles. The boys stepped off a few steps back toward the cliff that they had just come from earlier and fell from the cumbersome attached ankles.

"What'ya two idiots doin'?"

"It's hard to walk with our ankles tied."

"Well I left enough for the two of ya to walk with your legs stepping together. Now move!" The man was getting anxious, waving both his hands in front of him toward them to motion them on like cattle. However, though while Oggie tried to get up, Xavier just sat there examining the knots on the rope.

"What'ya doin' kid?"

"Just checking out that knot mister. That's some knot. It just gets tighter if ya pull on it. An' it hurts."

"Well boy, just get us to that camp and I'll fix it so it ain't so tight."

"Any ways you could loosen it a little, it's kind of cutting off the blood to my foot."

"Don't you be tryin' anythin', elst I'll cut your fool head off. Hear me?" With that he put his hand on a large knife in a sheath that was tucked into his belt at the waist, and though the boys could not see the blade, his ugly nature was enough to render it unsafe to disobey. When the man knelt to loosen the knot a little, Xavier offered facial expressions to Oggie and

156

nodded toward the cliff. Unable to read Xavier's head signs and not wanting to annoy that bad man, Oggie shrugged his head back and forth. Xavier then offered a few small hand signs over the mans head so that the man could not see them, in an attempt to tell Oggie to jump over the cliff when he (Xavier) did. Oggie shrugged his shoulders again just as the man looked up to see the boys' signs to each other.

"What'ya boys up to? I tell ya, I'd just soon cut you ta pieces as deal with the likes of you two, you hear me?"

"Please don't hurt us," pleaded Oggie, "we'll do anything you ask."

"Yea mister," agreed Xavier, "just what you gonna do with us after we get ya to the camp?"

"We'll just see about that there. For now, get movin'. I loosened the knot so no more complainin'. Get movin'." The boys started moving toward the cliff stumbling several times until they got the timing of pacing their legs next to each other together. While working their way toward the cliffs edge, Xavier kept looking for the vine which they had left hanging over the edge. Finally caught a view of the vine, he slowly veered the path to the right where it was, trying desperately not to make the slight change in direction noticeable; however, not very successful.

"Hey! Where you goin'?" Yelled the man. The boys stopped and turned toward him, placing them about twenty feet from the cliffs edge.

"Uh...." Xavier tried to think quickly.

"Answer me boy! Now!" The man approached them anxiously with a scowl on his face and placing his hand on the handle of the knife.

"Uh....I...ah....ah just wanted Oggie to see where he almost fell." Xavier's heart pounded with relief as his brow broke into a sweat.

"Well, forget it. Let's get a move on." The man nodded his head in the direction of where the cliff joined the woods, which is where Xavier had pointed to earlier as the spot that lead to the roadway.

"Please mister, it'll just take a sec."

"Fine. Just hurry or I'll push you boys over the edge. I need grub."

As they turned Xavier whispered down toward his chest, "When I say jump, jump."

Oggie tried to reciprocate the action, but not very successful, "what?"

"I said, when I say jump, jump."

"Are you outta your mind? We'll be killed."

"Naw, we'll jump on that ledge you and me climbed up on before." Oggie nodded his head in approval.

"What'ya boys talking about?"

"Ah...well.... ah just talking about the near fall a little while ago. Oggie's afraid of the height."

"No I'm not." Oggie pushed Xavier and the two fell because of the tied ankles. When they fell, they were at the edge.

"See you numskull," said Xavier to Oggie, "you coulda got us goin' down that hill to our deaths again."

"What'da'ya mean, again?"

"Well hadn't it been for you wantin' to climb the dumb thing in the beginning, we wouldn'ta nearly fell to our deaths before."

"Oh shut up!" Scolded Oggie.

"Yea! Both ya shut up!" The man was angry. "I'm sick'o'this! Now let's get movin'. Now!!" He hollered.

The boys got up on their knees and turned away from the man to finish getting up. They were right where the vine trailed over the edge. It was the spot where there were no ledges or rocks below them to cling too. With their backs toward the man, Xavier looked over the edge and lifting one hand off the ground, pushed Oggie's head in the direction of the valley below.

"See the ledge?" Xavier whispered. Oggie nodded affirmatively. "Let's start arguing and act like we're fighting, then when he comes over to grab us, jump down on that ledge over there," he nodded his head in the direction of the ledge they had climbed up from earlier.

"And if we're lucky he'll fall off." Xavier added with a softer whisper.

"You better be right Xav, or we're dead. You heard 'im."

"Yea, just pray it works."

"I'm prayin'. I'm prayin'."

"Hey stop the talk. You boys try anythin', and I'll slice you both into pieces! Hear me?" He shouted.

The boys started to get up. With one hand still on the ground, Xavier pushed Oggie's shoulder with his free hand.

"Was too your fault!" Xavier hollered pushing at Oggie.

Looking puzzled for a moment before the plan kicked in that slower mind of his Oggie spoke back almost like a rehearsed actor.

"Was not." The boys were now standing upright and pushing at each other and saying ugly things to each other, getting the attention of their kidnapper.

"Hey! You boys stop it!"

Startled by the interruption in their plan for a split second, the two looked in the direction of their kidnapper. However, realizing their mistake, they quickly turned back at their plan, when Xavier's eyes bugged out with a frightful look on his face and taking in a full lunged gasp of air. Oggie on the other hand, turned his head to look over the edge of the cliff to try to set their position expecting that they were about to jump.

"What'd'ya lookin' at kid?" The man started to turn his head and look behind him, but caught himself. "Oldest trick in the book boy. Not fallin' for it."

"Naaa...ah...ah...ahh" Xavier's voice was caught in shorted breaths and his eyes opened wide, even wider still. Oggie whispered that he was ready and kept his eyes on the point of landing.

"Look kid, I'm sick 'o this. I'm not turnin' to look. Get a move on." Xavier gasped a second breath and started to look pale.

"That's it!" The man shouted, "I've had about as much as I can take from you boys!" He began stepping closer to the boys. And, unlike Oggie figured, Xavier was planted solid in his tracks.

"We gonna jump?" Oggie whispered from the side of his mouth toward Xavier expecting to jump any second. The man was dangerously closing in on the boys' position and Xavier's lack of answer directed Oggie's curiosity to look at his pals face. With a flash, Oggie saw Xavier's wide-eyed pale fright and quickly turned his head in the direction of Xavier's view. Like his frightened and frozen pal, he too quickly drew in a full lung of air while his eyes stretched opened so wide and round that one could have driven a truck through such an opening. Both boys ears pressed back, in unison they both let loose with a full scaled holler.

"AAAAhhhhhhhhh!!!! AAAAhhhhhhhh!!"

CHAPTER 25

OH MY . . . !

"AAAAhhhhhh!! AAAhhhhh!!!!" Screamed Xavier and Oggie again in unison as if on cue to scream at the tops of their voices. Just the shrill of the two boys screams was enough to force anyone to look, but their adrenalin driven scream gave way to the man deciding he should at the very least glance behind him. So he did. Just a glancing flash over his shoulder at first with his body remaining forward toward the boys, then swinging his head back forward. His body began to shake and couldn't believe his memory. Moreover, what he saw couldn't really have been. So, he turned his head again, this time turning his body half way around to gain a better view of what it was he had seen.

"AAAhhhhhhh!!!!" The boys screamed again; and yet again. Startled, the man jerked his head back toward the boys then again to his attacker.

"AAAhhhhhhh!!!" The boys screamed behind him only heightening the level of shock and terror. Seeing his lurching attacker straight on, he stepped backward a couple steps with the hope of grabbing one or both of the boys and force them between him and the oncoming horror that was certain to come. However, as he reached back behind him and then glanced to where the boys were supposed to be, they were not there. Having seen a window of time where the man was occupied, the boys had already tumbled, not jumped like they had planned, but tumbled down to the ledge below.

Not seeing the boys, the man turned his back to the ledge and pulled the knife from his waist, holding it securely and waving it profusely in the air. The attacker stood upright as the man inched backwards still waving the knife, while, about ten feet below him, the boys heard the rustle of sticks and branches on the ground followed by a loud, soul penetrating, roar which they had never heard before ever in their lives. Right then, both boys wished from the very depths of their souls, their most innermost being that they weren't experiencing any of this. Again came another ear shrilling roar.

"GGGGGGRRRRRRRR!!!!" It was unmistakable to anyone who would have been within earshot of its' majesty. The Black Bear! A most fearful and dreaded animal of the forest and right this moment Xavier and Oggie were hearing it in the wild, along with a criminal who they now heard. Moreover, this bear just happened to be one of the largest ever recorded.

"GO AWAY!!!" The man screamed and yelled at the huge 700 pound bear profusely; which only seemed to encourage the responding roar each time.

"GRRAAAWWWW!!!! GRRRRRRAWWWWWW!!!!"

The boys were huddled almost into a small shaking ball on the ledge with their heads buried in the rocks and dirt with their hands over the back of their necks as Xavier had instructed quickly the moment they were in place on the ledge and thus covering the area where blood comes the closest to the surface of the skin, and blood being the attraction for bears. They feared being eaten alive. 'How could they live?' They each thought separately. Mentally they screamed the same prayer, at almost the same time, 'Oh God save us!'

"GRRRRRRR!!!!" The roars were getting closer evidencing that the attacker was after his target, and just above them. They dared not look up to see their deaths, but preferred it come by surprise. The man yelled at the bear and some scurrying was heard above them in the sticks and foliage, followed by, falling rocks and gravel trickling on top of them.

"AAAAHHHHhhhhh!!" They heard as the voice of the man faded first above them then fading down below them, evidencing that the convict had fallen from the cliff in his attempt to get clear of the attacking bear. Trembling, they huddled their bodies tighter against each other and began forcing the air out of their lungs as they emotionally cried out in their silence, trying to listen over their pounding thuds of fear in their chest, their brain, and even in their necks as their hearts raced to explode from fear.

Any moment and they would feel the strike against their small frames, the claws dig into their skin or feel the heat of the fierce creatures mouth as it prepared to bite its' teeth into their skin and feel its' jaw clamp down on their skin and feel their bones break under this ferocious animals strength. In fact, if the animals swinging strike alone were not enough, its' contact would certainly knock them over the edge wherein the fall would cease their existence.

Suddenly, a few pebbles trickled down from above them manifesting their attackers presence causing their bodies to shake so hard it was all they could do to hold their position and not vibrate right straight off the edge. For a fleeting split second Xavier thought, 'If only I hadn't thought up this stupid idea, we wouldn't be in this mess. I'm so sorry,' he wanted to tell Oggie, however, Oggie was in his own state of fear knowing that he would never see his mom or dad ever again. Xavier thought for a moment they should go ahead and jump, after all they might survive the fall with only a bunch of broken bones but at least they would be alive. He was just starting to tell Oggie of the plan, when his entire brain was shaken nearly out of its skulled enclosure.

"GRRRRRAAAAAA!!! GRRRRRAAAAWWWWW!!!" The game had changed and the machine had tilted; the game was over. Each boy prepared to feel the claws rip into their backs, to feel teeth slicing into their skin and ripping away a chunk of flesh, together the boys cried inside so hard they swore they could feel their body's pouring out blood through their tears.

"KAPOW!!" They heard a loud bolt echo and roar across the valley originating from somewhere above them.

"KAPOW!!" Again it boomed like an explosive. Above them plenty of rock and debris fell and rolled onto their backs causing them to scream harder if that were even possible.

"AAAhhhhhhhh!!!" They couldn't even hear their own screams because their brains had checked out; and, even greater fear had fully arrived and taken over; they were nearly to black out in fear. It was soon to be over.

CHAPTER 26

NOW WHAT?

"You boys O.K.?" It was a man's voice, but unlike that of the man who had kidnapped them.

Xavier barely turned his head upward and peeked up to his left. It was a police officer standing on the grassy ledge above them. What a welcoming sight.

"Oh No!" Xavier screamed in fear. His hands scrambled like a wild animal in the sand and gravel on the ledge trying to get some kind of grip so that he could climb the four to six feet or so to the landing above them. The two boys grabbed at and clung on to each other as they tried to stand although, their aggravated weakness was preventing them from being much of any kind of stable.

"Hold on," rushed the police officer, "I'll help 'ya." He knelt down and reached his long arm to their reaching arms and upon connecting; they nearly pulled him over the edge. Their rush to the top was second only to their gasping for breath. Upon the police officer dragging them away from the edge, Oggie eventually passed out completely, and Xavier gasped for air profusely nearly regurgitating several times. The officer rolled Oggie onto his back and freed his tee shirt so as to watch the boys' chest and stomach to insure that the lad was breathing.

"Your not....," Xavier gasped out between breaths, "gonna believe....what happened." He took several deep breaths.

"Take your time son, we have all day. Take some deep breaths," instructed the officer. The police officer stood upright and started toward the edge of the cliff, Xavier grabbed his pant leg.

"Where you goin'? Please don't leave?" Xavier pleaded.

"Just going to the ledge to see what happened to the convict. You're all right, the bear headed over there," said he pointing toward the roadway where the cliff edge and road up from the valley below met. Xavier let loose but watched every step, getting less comfortable when the police officer reached the cliffs edge to gaze a look below, and then more comfortable upon the police officers return, along with his weapon that chased the bear away.

"Don't think he's goin' anywhere. In fact, looks like he's alive but for sure at least two broken legs at the very least. He'll wish he'd never broke out."

"Oh thank God! It's you, Chief Malcum!" Xavier's eye muscles began to gain control and his focus began to come into view. He had squeezed his eyes so tight that the blood had departed the focusing muscles, preventing focal awareness.

"Well, you just might want to thank him for your safety."

"Oh I do! I do!" Xavier repeated his thanks to God for saving them several times verbally and many times more mentally.

"What was that kaboom?" Asked Xavier.

"Oh I shot my revolver to signal our position and to chase away your little friend."

Xavier wished that the Chief hadn't mentioned the bear, for he had just about forgotten the event for just a second and the fear around the event that dug deep into his soul.

"Oh God," pleaded the boy beginning to break into tears. Chief Malcum leaned forward and took the young lad in his arms. Xavier wrapped his arms around the Chief as if his life depended upon the hold.

"Now there Xavier, everything is O.K." He patted the young lad on the back to console his damaged emotion. Xavier fought his tears, not wanting the Chief to see him this way.

"Your O.K. buddy. Some experience you guys had here." The Chief pushed at Xavier's side to push him away a bit.

"Hey, saw that camp site of yours. Quite a set up." The Chief pointed out confidently. Xavier leaned back some and dropped his head to hide his emotion.

"Yea, coons got us last night," responded Xavier wiping tears from his cheekbones with the back of his right hand.

"Yes sir, I saw that. Smart of you to burn the remainder. Them things carry rabies you know." It was a statement, but was also a question to confirm Xavier's knowledge.

"Yes sir, my grandpa tole me that." Xavier thought about his grandpa and how he wished he were here right now. Just then Oggie stirred.

"You O.K. son?" Asked the Chief.

"Huh?" Sounded Oggie cracking his eyes open and rolling his eyeballs up in his head; then continuing, "Huh..Wha?"

Oggie took several shallow breaths and barely rolled to the right and regurgitated, doubling his knees up and leaning his head toward them.

"What's wrong?" Asked his concerned friend Xavier.

"Shock, Xavier. He'll be all right in just a second." Chief Malcum placed his hand upon Oggie's forehead and stroked the boys' hair back as his hand moved from front to back. He continued to stroke the boys' head several times.

"Wha..." Oggie gasped, "wha...happen?"

"We're O.K. Og!" Xavier was regaining his own strength.

"Oh no Xav." Faintly voiced the weak young lad as he pushed his face down in the grass, squinting his eyes hard.

"Oh no!" The boy broke into tears. "It was awful. It had big teeth. Oh No; no!"

The Chief continued stroking the forehead and top of Oggie's head.

"You're all right son. God knows. Hey, that your army canteen back there at the camp?" The Chief worked to get Oggie's mind working on something else. He also knew that one day they'd look back on this and he wanted them to feel like young men rather then scared little puppies, so he focused on getting them up and into action, like normal if that were possible after such an *ordeal*.

"Where's.... that...ah...guy?" Asked Oggie selecting his words slowly and carefully.

"He's done gone down the hill you almost did, Oggie," reported Xavier.

"Really?" Oggie perked up a little straightening out and lifting his head to look at his pal.

"Yepper," his now mildly recovered friend shot back.

"He hurt?"

"Oh yea. Chief says he's broke up pretty bad."

"You mean he's not dead?" Said Oggie with an enthusiasm of amazement.

"Not at all."

"See Xav?" Said he lifting up on one arm, and then settling back down when he quickly got light headed.

"See what?" Asked Xavier.

"See, I told ya we was in no danger climbin' that hill."

"You boys climbed that hill?" Chief Malcum inquired.

"Yes sir," quickly replied Xaiver, "right there where the vines hangin' over the edge. Had to get it to save Oggie from falling when he slipped."

"I don't think we oughta tell your folks about that guys."

"Why not," questioned Oggie trying to lift up again.

"Well, I think this adventure with the criminal and the *visitor* is sufficient to scare your folks into a frenzy. Let alone add the survival of the big cliff. What'd ya think?"

"Yeah you're right!" Exclaimed Xaiver quickly, then turning to Oggie.

"What Chief Malcum is sayin' Og, is that if we tell 'em more than they need, we'll be grounded from doin' things like this again forever." Xavier added.

"That's fine!" Exclaimed Oggie, as he lifted himself up on one elbows, "I don't plan on ever doin' anything like this ever again."

"O.K lads, I can see that we've gained enough energy to head back toward our *rendezvous* with the camp." Chief Malcum added standing up and helping Oggie slowly rise to a vertical position in stages since the little heavy set fellow was still occasionally light headed.

"Yea, let's *rendezvous*," added Xavier.

The Chief gazed over the edge of the cliff for a moment then turned toward the boys and put his hand on their shoulders as the three of them began their trip toward camp.

"He still there?" Asked Oggie.

"Oh yea. Not goin' anywhere, that's for sure." Just then a branch cracked off to their right. Both boys instantly grabbed the Chief from either side and wrapping their arms around his side and waist so tight he could hardly breathe.

"Boys," pressed the Chief, "it's just a trooper over there." He pointed to their right. They looked in the direction of his finger, and sure enough, there was another police officer.

"Down over the hill!" Hollered the Chief at the police officer, "I think he's injured pretty bad."

"Got it!" The other officer replied.

"Well, someone else sorta took care of the business for us." Shouted the Chief.

"The boys?" Inquired the officer.

"Naw," the Chief paused, "someone *much* bigger."

"Oh him." The Chief and other police officer nodded their heads at each other and smiled.

Xavier looked up at the Chief, then at the officer.

"I think God was part of the whole process too," added Xavier. With a puzzled look, the police officer looked at Chief Malcum, the two pushed their large rimmed hats back and nodded their heads up and down with a smiling frown as the State Police officer headed in the direction of the cliff.

"You can get down by the road on the left side of the cliff," hollered Xavier.

"Thanks son," replied the officer.

"We'll send back help," added the Chief.

"Thanks," sounded the fading voice.

The Chief and the two boys resumed the walk through the forest in the direction of the camp.

"Whew!" Exclaimed Xavier wiping sweat from his forehead in disgust.

"This has sure been some camping trip." He added.

"I'd call it an adventure, Xavier." Chuckled Chief Malcum.

"Yea, I guess so," agreed Xavier.

"Well for me it was a nightmare!" Exclaimed Oggie.

The three looked each other back and forth then all three laughed.

CHAPTER 27

EPILOG

Over the next few hours, the boys were escorted to their folks for one happy reunion to say the least. Plenty of tears were shed as 'JOY' filled the room and hearts at the Winfield home. Both criminals had been recovered, the one having collected two broken legs, four broken ribs, a broken arm, and fractured collarbone in three places, not to mention a concussion, and the other nearly expired from bee stings when the two stumbled into a honeybee nest trying to navigate through the lower basin thicket field.

"I think the two criminals will be happy to get back to prison," stated Chief Malcum.

"I'll say," added Oggie; then, "I can't believe he lived."

"Well Xavier, what have you learned from all this?" Asked Chief Malcum, who had joined the Winfield's and Bartholomew's at the Winfield home upon having completed the necessary paper work and saying his goodbye's to the State Police.

The boy thought for a moment.

"Well first, I guess I'll make sure to tell my folks exactly what I'm doin' next time, and in detail with map and direction. Then second, I guess I'll make sure to check the news to see if it's actually safe." The group chuckled at the young lads fearless aura.

"And you?" Asked the Chief of Oggie.

"Well...." he thought tilting his head a little back and to the right, "I ain't goin' campin' in the woods without an adult, and I ain't listenin' to Xavier, no more."

The entire group broke into laughter, the Chief included.

"Well boys, without a doubt you've had an experience than none of us could top, but I am to wonder," continued the Chief's questioning, "What on earth will you think of next?"

Xavier and Oggie looked at each other and tilted their heads in suspicion. The room was silent awaiting their answer. But neither of them could think of anything to say. What could top what had just happened to them.

Breaking the silence, "I was thinking of trying to trap lightning in a jar or a rod or something," concluded Xavier. The group gasped in amazement.

"Oh no your not!" Exclaimed Grandma Winfield shaking her head back and forth swiftly.

"O.K." Agreed the young lad, following which there was this sported healthy round of chuckles and laughs.

"How about a long bike ride? To say.... Cumberland (a town about 50 miles away)?" Suggested Oggie.

"No Way!" Shouted Mrs. Bartholomew jokingly pointing her finger at him as if to be scolding.

"But," inserted Xavier turning to his grandpa, "look at what we will be able to tell our children and grandchildren when reflecting on our childhood?"

The old man looked down at the boy, shook his head back and forth, and tugged Xavier close to his side.

"Well Xavier, knowing you and Oggie, I think the two of you will have plenty of adventures to share with your children and grandchildren, including this one."

As neighbor to the Winfield's and having been there present that day, I added my own two cents.

"In fact Xavier, it wouldn't surprise me one bit if some day I'd see a story or even a book by the very title, *The Adventures of Xavier Winfield*." To which, grandma Winfield lifted her finger in the air.

"And don't forget His Pal Oggie," she added.

"Sure," said I, "*and His Pal Oggie.*"

So that's how it was, those adventurous few days that hot summer in Chestnut Ridge following the arrival of Xavier Winfield to Chestnut Ridge. And to think, *The Great Camping Experience* was just the beginning. I heard someone once say, 'today is the first day of the rest of your life.' Well, for Xavier and Oggie, no truer words could be spoken; because for them, every day was another opportunity to explore life's richness and adventure. You see, for those two adventurous boys, adventure was just another day and another time. So, thanks for listening to my story, and hope we get to meet for another little chat again soon. Oh, by the way - - next time ask me about, "*The Great Train Ride.*"

THE END

GLOSSARY

acclaimed – (EH-claim-da) – to announce, proclaim, or give notice to something or someone special, as in heralding them to be well known or celebrity.

alcove – (AL-kov) – a small indentation or pocket along a wall, corridor, or line or stack of items.

endearment – (INN-deer-mint) – to term special with feelings, as in a special person or thing, more specifically as in people; like a special feeling about a person.

escapades – (S-cah-paids) – doing some thing that involves action, travel, or adventure

excavation – (X-cah-vaa-shun) – a cut away portion of land or soil or earth that is cut with machinery like as in where bull dozer cuts away at the ground where a house is being building.

experimented – (X-peer-eh-min-tud) – to experiment or test or try several times something out, as in trying this, then that, and then another or more times which is the plural of experiment.

gelatin – (GEL-eh-ton) – a rubbery like dessert like jello.

judgment – (JAHJ-mint) – to pass a decision or thought of decision toward someone or something; as in passing an opinion about someone or something.

loam – (LOW-mm) – a soft easy to break up kind of soil, sometimes in the form of sandy, clay, and mixed with earth or rocks or sand.

maneuvered – (MAH-new-ver-dah) – to steer, guide, or move something from one place to another.

maturity – (mah-chur-eh-tee) – showing of age, as in not a child but as in a teen or adult be it decisions or actions.

obligated – (AHB-lah-gate-tud) – must do something that is to be done as in responsibility to do something or carry out some task or purpose.

ordeal – (ORR-deel) – and extremely or very trying test or happening

paraphernalia – (pear-eh-fah-NAIL-yah) – gear, equipment, packages of stuff, stuff, pieces, parts, or a pile of things.

proverbial – (pro-ver-BEE-ul) – written or stated words that mean such as or like to be known as in always known or guessed to be known.

rendezvous – (RON-day-voo) – a French word meaning to meet up with someone as in a time and place

serenity – (seh-WREN-eh-tee) – quiet, no noise, silent

stupor – (STEW-pur) – knocked out completely or almost as in dizzy, half lost mentally and can't seem to get ones baring or location or like half asleep.

supposition (sup-oh-zish-un) – to suppose something or make a conclusion as to what one things might be the answer, or conclusion, or idea.

tendered – (TEN-der-dah) – handed to, given to, offered to, or hired as in a job or responsibility like handing off something from one person to another or offering to them something.

vehemently – (VEE-uh-munt-lee) – with strong meaning or emphasis, as in really really meaning something with no way out.

zeal – (ZEE-ell) – with meaning and energy as to get up and do something when one is tired and would rather just sit.

The Adventures of Xavier Winfield
and his pal Oggie Series

*In Episode Two the adventure continues involving a train,
a chase, and making it one totally explosive episode!*

*In Episode Three a new explorer joins the duo, creating
conflict
for the boys, but will Xavier allow 'her' take the lead?*

*To learn more about each episode and release dates,
visit your local book retailer or visit . .*
www.xavierwinfield.com

To Learn More About The Adventure Team
visit . . .

www.xavierwinfield.com

backpack publishers
www.backpackpublishers.com